STEPHANIE

Susanna Hughes

First published in Great Britain in 1991
by Nexus Books
338 Ladbroke Grove
London W10 5AH

Copyright © Susanna Hughes 1991

Typeset by Medcalf Type Ltd, Bicester, Oxon.
Printed and bound in Great Britain by
Cox & Wyman Ltd, Reading, Berks.

ISBN 0 352 32793 6

This book is sold under the condition that it shall not, by way of trade or otherwise, be lent, re-sold, hired out or otherwise circulated in any form of binding or cover other than that in which it is published, and without a similar condition including this condition being imposed on the subsequent purchaser.

1

One night she dreamt about him. Dreamt, not crudely, not pornographically, that he was in her, having her, breaking her. Dreamt not of wet phallus, ruthless penetration, rhythmically plunging buttocks, but of passion. Of him and passion. Of lust and passion abstracted from flesh and blood; a dream of emotion, of feeling with no images, a dream of sexual satisfaction without sexual mechanics. Satisfaction centred on him. Emotion and feeling centred on him. Emotion and feeling totally concerned with sex. A subconscious presentation of how much her body craved and wanted him.

Stephanie could not remember if the dream had come before she had bought the book, the first of the books, or after. It seemed that both had occurred simultaneously but, of course, one did have to come first. (Much later she knew the books had come before the dream.) Not that it really mattered. At the moment, after all, only he seemed to matter.

She had watched Martin now for several weeks. She watched him come in and sit down in the mornings. It was late summer and he never wore a coat. She watched his thighs. She watched his face. She thought she knew how his arms looked, how his legs and buttocks were shaped, how his muscles would lie when he stretched out, how they would contract when he moved. She knew his face, she knew his expressions. She knew the way creases appeared on his face if he worried, frowned or smiled. She watched the smallest changes that flitted across his brow and thought she could recognise every emotion, every nuance of emotion.

He paid little attention to her. He knew her name, but that was inevitable and she could take no comfort from the fact. He would say good morning and good night but there was no reason for him to say anything else to her. Their work did not bring them together. They had no friends in common. Their lives were separate, joined only by the open-plan office. She had calculated the distance to his desk, one empty day. Sixteen feet. She had converted it to metres. She had added on four feet to cover the distance from the edge of the desks to the chairs on which they both sat. Twenty feet. That had made her cross all evening. Cross at her schoolgirl passion, cross at such ridiculous calculations. Cross at him. Cross at his lack of awareness.

She had never conceived such feelings before. Such desire. Such unrequited desire. Why now? Why here and now? She was conscious of the amount of time she spent thinking about Martin, dreaming about Martin, seeing Martin. She was conscious that he had become larger than life, better than life: stronger, more than real.

Perhaps she didn't want him at all. Perhaps the fantasy was the attraction and the reality would be a grubby disappointment. It was a comforting thought. She had read that the essence of sexual pleasure was fantasy: so this was her fantasy. As George laboured at her body and her mind lifted away to Martin it was true she became aroused in a way George had never been able to arouse her unless she imagined he was Martin. His thigh, his eyes, his hands, his penis.

George was conscientious sexually when the mood took him (if the mood took him). For two years on an occasional basis he had made love to her conscientiously. He had given her orgasms when she was in the mood. She had faked orgasms when she wasn't. He was clean and pleasant and, she supposed, she would have ultimately allowed him to take her over. She would sink into his comfortable life. Her comfortable family in their comfortable home had sent her to a comfortable school and a comfortable university. And then comfortable George had found her or she had found him, she couldn't remember which, and they would continue the comfortable circle with comfortable children of their own. That was it, she told herself. That was what this sudden passion was all about – an adolescent middle-class desire for adventure, excitement, perhaps even a desire to punish herself for the guilt of possessing so much comfort. (Was that psychological sophistication running riot?) Unfortunately such thoughts did not lessen the passion nor make it more bearable.

George lay next to her now, his erect penis pushing against her thigh as his mouth sucked on her nipple. The first sticky drops of Cowper's fluid leaking from his penis felt tacky on the flesh of her navel. She was not in the mood. His tongue flicked at the point of her nipple, then circled it, leaving a wet trail on her breast. She could think only of the trails slugs leave on garden paths. She felt his hand running down from her back over her other breast and then on to her navel. Rather too quickly she thought. She knew exactly what he would do next. The inevitable routine. His hand ran on down to her knee, caressing it perfunctorily before moving up again along the inside of her thigh. Cue for his mouth to seek her neck. His hand pushed down into her downy pubic hair to find her clitoris. This time she allowed him to part her thighs but with rather more effort than usual so his movements seemed harsher, clumsier. That minor game played, once his fingertip had found her clitoris, she separated her legs with better grace and gave a little, almost imperceptible, moan. He was in a hurry. His fingers hardly paused at her clitoris before they dived to find her opening. She knew what he would find: she was dry and unyielding. No room for passion.

George's conscientiousness overcame his disappointment. His fingers stroked the long crease of her sex, starting at the top of her clitoris and plunging along to the knot of her arse. Every time she sensed a pause at her vagina as if he was testing the temperature of the water. She remained passive. She was not in the mood. Now he concentrated on the little bud of her clitoris, caressing it slowly, regularly. Nine points for effort. The sensation of pleasure reached up to her. She sensed her body arching towards him. She knew the wetness was growing in her vagina, just as she could feel the wetness seeping from his penis down on to the flesh of her thigh. Another slug's trail. He moved on to her, his penis rubbing the curls of her pubic hair but she was not ready: his penetration was clumsy. Her vagina resisted as he pushed inside. Half resisted. The head of his penis was received but he could get no further without hurting her. He wanted entry and would not retreat. She gasped as he pushed into her. He whispered his apology but pushed again: this time he said, 'sorry' with the same inflection as 'fuck you'.

Raising her head slightly over his shoulder she could see the rise and fall of his arse. He had a spot, red and ugly, on the top of his left buttock. The movement of his penis inside her moved her not at all. The excitement that lubricated her vagina was automatic, a reflex. The body had no reflex for pleasure once penetration was achieved. That was the mind's job. He had started kissing her neck again but his mouth was too wet and she felt saliva run down to the pillow. She was conscious of his weight. She was aware that the distance between this activity and ecstasy was very small. She knew how to cover that distance but tonight she would not. She would not think of Martin. She would not imagine him. She would not.

George's weight was getting too much for her. Callously, like the white-coated man she had once seen pushing the stallion's penis into a mare, she reached under his thighs with her hand and took hold of his balls. At first she could only hold one, the other bounced out of her reach; but by pulling on the skin of his scrotum she reeled the other into her grasp. So vulnerable, she thought, cupped in her hand. George's movements increased as it always did. She pulled harder, pulling his balls away from his penis. Milking time. She felt him come with her hand, his balls tightening as he groaned and pushed into her. She made no attempt to come or to pretend to come.

Perhaps it was the ordinariness of her sex with George that had made her buy the first book. Not consciously though. In fact now she couldn't remember where she had bought it, even if she had bought it or if someone — who, she could not imagine — had given it to her.

In fact it was like the chicken and the egg: which had come first — her curiosity about sex or the book which had created her curiosity? Curiosity did not seem an appropriate word. It was not like wanting to find out how many types of butterfly there were. At least it was not like that now. Now curiosity had turned to fascination. And fascination was turning to something else. She had read the book casually at first, not paying much attention to it. But after she'd read it she realised that some of the things she'd read kept coming back to her, drifting into a vacant mind, even a busy mind. She read it again.

The man's penis had been bound in a leather strap around his balls and the base of his erection. The strap made the penis swell, each vein engorged with blood standing out in relief like the branches of dead ivy wrapped round a fallen tree.

When she was alone, after George had expressed his guilt at her not coming, at his haste, and after she made some excuse as to why he couldn't spend the night in her bed, she did not fall asleep. The idea of Martin demanded her attention. She had not wanted it earlier for some reason, but now she was not sure. If she allowed it she would become aroused, if she did not she would have to try to sleep. Martin. She thought of Martin, and then cut him from her mind with the thought of George and the red spot on his plunging buttock. The image was like a cold shower. Then she thought of Martin again. The water became hotter. Her hand moved to her clitoris. She must not. She must not. He must not. He must not dominate her. What schoolgirl fantasies. She was a woman behaving like a child; she must exclude him. She must not allow him to become a shibboleth of her actions.

Her fingers had found their own rhythm. Her vagina was wet from George's semen. Her fingers slid easily from her vagina to her clitoris, to the knot of her clitoris as she wallowed in sensation. She held the door open for Martin as she parted her legs, as she threw back the sheets for him. She did everything for Martin. Her fingers explored for him, touched for him, felt for him. She moaned as if he would hear. She cried out as if he would hear. She felt the juices flow inside her as he would feel them. She came then, sharply, almost painfully. In the aftermath she felt no chill in the warmth she had generated. No regret that she had allowed in. He had taken her. He had forced her. She was not to blame.

2

Stephanie didn't really panic until twelve. At ten-thirty she imagined him sitting in his car on the West Way, reading a newspaper, waiting for the traffic in front of him to unsnarl itself. At eleven-thirty the traffic jam theory was altogether too preposterous: it had to be something else, something she could not imagine. At twelve she panicked. The chair twenty feet away remained empty. It was not until lunch time that she discovered he had been moved upstairs.

Another girl had heard from his secretary, the one he had shared but who was now going to be exclusively his, that he had been promoted one grade. One grade, one floor; the company believed in symmetrical neatness in matters of status. The top floor was the *top* floor.

It was difficult to analyse her feelings. In a sense she felt relief, in a sense disappointment. In a sense she felt gratitude. It would be a relief not to stare continually, to be continually reminded of her desire and distance between them. A relief from his physical presence. It was a disappointment not to be able to see him, not to be able to top up her images of him with the reality: to add to her images the sort of shirt he was wearing and the kind of tie. The gratitude was more complex and perhaps quite out of place. The company that had moved him upstairs was to be thanked if it made it easier for her to reach him, if the fact that they were no longer in proximity would mean an affair could now be started without embarrassment.

She had gone over to him so many times in her imagination, with so many different approaches that she sometimes found it difficult to remember that she had never actually spoken to him. And in those imagined dialogues he had often explained to her that he couldn't become involved with someone he worked with, however remotely. It would be too distracting for them, too much to bear. At least this line of defence against her was now partly closed. One less excuse for him to fall back on.

The afternoon passed. The desk remained empty. Her head remained full; full of new approaches, new avenues, new adventures, new circumstances. She had known that if circumstances had remained unchanged it would have taken her weeks to approach him across those twenty feet: now she knew it would take her only days to go up one floor, find his desk and speak to him. Speak to Martin. Only a few days now. It only remained to rehearse exactly what she would say and exactly what he would do.

George took her out to dinner at the weekend. She had almost decided that Monday was to be the day. She would allow George to distract her once more. Next week might be another world. And of course, realistically, absolutely nothing might change – in which case George, stringy and full of holes, would serve as her safety net.

He liked Japanese food. The waitresses, obis

indicating their innocence, serve the man first, bowing and backing away. She was sure it was this rather than the delicate, intricately prepared food that appealed to George. The women were so small, so self-effacing, so undemanding; any one of them would be the perfect wife for the perfect chauvinist. George always attempted some Japanese greeting which produced refined giggles whenever it was trotted out. The women smiled and smiled and smiled. If they thought him a fool they showed not the slightest sign of it. If they sat behind the paper screens in the kitchen, telling each other how he mispronounced their language and laughing at his presumptions, by the time they returned with the food their faces had been wiped of any expression save their innocuous smiles.

George insisted they drunk sake. She found it cloying, especially when the heat had left it, and it always left a strange numbing aftertaste in her mouth, as if she had just paid a visit to the dentist.

In a way the food had the same effect. Her mouth felt used, her teeth ached slightly as though their enamel had been coated with some fine acid. Over tea, while George ordered more sake, she listened to the conversation on the next table. It was occupied by a couple, the man in his fifties with a ragged careworn face, who spoke English with a heavy middle-European accent, and the girl no more than twenty with an almost pure white complexion. Everything about the girl suggested innocence, not sexual innocence, but innocence of life, sin, of hurt. The man told her, his voice lowered, of a previous affair with a girl who had worked in the British Embassy in Bucharest. He was trying to shock her, to hurt her a little: his tone was hard almost angry. She remained placid, ahead of the game through her innocence. Eventually she asked whether the girl had been a good lover. The man did not answer. What happened to her, the girl continued. She married a Major in the infantry.

George finished his sake and took her home. The image of the white-skinned girl laying naked before the older man grew in her mind. She would be slightly overweight, but only slightly: just too rounded. He would be ugly. Ugly flesh. Ugly body. Ugly flesh driving into her softness. He would be a bad lover, coming too quickly, careless of feelings, his penis shrinking from her wet and wrinkled. He would not bother to make excuses.

They drove to her flat in silence. George came in without asking and poured himself a Scotch. When he kissed her the smell of his breath seemed to pour into her like a drink. She could find no way to prevent it. He kissed her with his tongue, pushing it up against her teeth and down into her mouth. Leaving him to undress, she went to the bathroom. The fluorescent light was uncompromising and exactly what she wanted. Almost with a physical shock, she realised she had not thought of Martin for two hours. She peed in a hard stream and took her make-up off, keeping her long dark hair out of the way with an old scarf. As she used the mirror she did not look at herself but merely what she was working on. The face that stared back at her seemed remote, impersonal, another woman, someone else. With the make-up removed she pulled her hair free from the scarf and shook her head. In the mirror the long black hair cascaded over her face. She pulled it back with one hand and stared hard at herself. Dark hair, deep brown eyes ('brandy eyes'), dark hairy eyebrows that had to be plucked regularly, long eyelashes, a small well-shaped nose and her mouth, her best feature; lips that were so dark they needed little lipstick, full fleshy lips in a sensual mouth. She suddenly felt cold and decided to leave her clothes on. She wondered about the girl with the white skin and remembered her saying to the man, 'I'm sorry I'm not very talkative.'

George was lying on the bed, on top of the bed naked. His penis was flaccid. On the bedside table was another glass of Scotch. She turned the other lights off, leaving just the light from the bedside lamp. He looked at his watch.

'It's Sunday.'

She did not reply.

Kneeling by his side on the bed, still fully clothed, she took his penis in her hand. He moved his head to look at her but otherwise did not move. Not conscientious tonight. He made no effort to kiss her. He made no effort to pull her down to him. He just watched her face. His penis began to swell in her hand. She had ringed it between her thumb and finger, and was drawing this ring up and down his shaft. When his penis had grown sufficiently, she stopped to pull back his foreskin so that her fingers touched the more sensitive ridges underneath. He made no noise but she could feel his penis swelling again. As she continued the slow movements she wished she had taken off her tights. Kneeling on them pulled at the nylon, making the position uncomfortable.

She stopped and got up off the bed. George looked momentarily alarmed and then perhaps disappointed as she reached up under her dress and pulled her tights and panties off. She took her dress off too but left her bra on.

When she resumed wanking him he looked happier, she thought. He did not want to fuck her, he hadn't the energy to fuck her, he did not want to perform.

She performed. Again she felt the urge to finish it quickly. She could take him in her mouth, holding his balls in her hand, squeezing him like an icing bag until the icing spilt into her mouth. She could but she would not. She moved her hand slightly so her thumb slid over the escarpment at the back of his penis. With her other hand she felt under his balls until her finger lay at the edge of his arse. Increasing the rhythm again she penetrated his anus with her middle finger feeling the dry warmth inside. His arse was not like a vagina; it was narrow and thin and clenched. As best she could she moved her finger to and fro, in and out, her finger a miniature penis. It had the desired effect. She watched as the eye of his penis opened and spat out his semen, hot and white, on to the back of her hand.

He closed his eyes and slept. She cupped the semen in her hands and went to the bathroom to wash it away. The semen clung tenuously to the bottom of the sink before finally giving in to the currents of water that surrounded it. She wiped the bowl with the cleaning cloth she kept under the sink and resisted the temptation to wipe it again with liquid cleaner. She took off her bra and looked at the marks it had made in the flesh of her large breasts. Her nipples had not been stirred by George; they were still flaccid. Despite their size, her breasts were taut, firm, always pointed upwards, defying gravity. She looked at her slim body, her long legs, fine pinched ankles, her tiny waist, the sprawl of black pubic hair which like her eyebrows — had she not trimmed regularly — would have spread up her navel and down her thighs. Martin. She combed her hair. Monday. Martin Monday.

The floor above was like the floor below; a little brighter and with fewer desks but with the same hard cord carpet, the same curved screens separating area from area, the same chairs, ashtrays and typewriters. She knew exactly what he would say to her and she knew whatever he said would be a surprise.

Martin was sitting at his desk.

'Hello.'

He looked up. Stephanie had seen him this close before, in the lifts, in the canteen, but never looking at her directly. His eyes were so brown they were almost as black as his hair. He said nothing.

'I came to congratulate you.'

His expression changed slightly. She read the new arrangement of his features, and tried to work out their meaning. He knows I didn't come to congratulate him: he knows I came to ask him to fuck me.

'Thank you.'

'I'd like to take you out to lunch.'

'To congratulate me?'

'No.'

'What then?' His expression changed again: she detected interest.

'May I?'

'I will take you.'

'That's not the point.'

'I know.'

They settled on the place and time. He dismissed her with a polite smile. She walked across the floor feeling self-conscious about her ankles, wondering if her hair was still tidy, wondering if he was even bothering to look at her ankles or her hair.

He ordered fish, she meat. The restaurant was not crowded. She was not nervous at being with him — she felt she had known him for a long time. He told her stories from his life. He told her stories that made her smile and sad stories that he told her seriously, letting her see the hurt in his eyes. (Real hurt?) He had an ability to use words in a way she had not come across before, to create places, people, ideas, from words. He talked in complete sentences, rarely letting himself be distracted into not finishing what he had begun to say. Parenthesised remarks were never allowed to develop beyond their original position. It was an accomplished act, honed down to the essentials, she imagined, by repeated performances.

She listened, mostly. She answered his questions about herself as truthfully as she felt she could, but he asked her nothing that touched her. He did not ask her why she had sought him out. He made no reference to her invitation. It was as though this lunch had been planned for some days: a meeting of old friends. Old friends who knew nothing of each other.

As he talked, she watched his eyes and his face as she had used to watch them from twenty feet away. The darting images that formed and re-formed on his face were like the changing shapes of clouds on a gusty windblown day. And yet his eyes remained curiously passive, as though they took little account of the proceedings. They looked at her steadily throughout the meal. She felt he had seen nothing else since they had sat down: his eyes never moved from her.

He ate very little, and drunk very little wine. It never occurred to her that she should follow his example: she ate with gusto and drunk most of the wine.

'Have you ever been married?' he asked her.

'No.'

'Involved?'

'At the time it felt as though I was. Looking back I can't say I really cared.' And she had almost forgotten it now, it was so long ago.

'Cared?' The word sounded strange the way he used it.

'In love.'

'I see.'

'Am I allowed to ask the same questions?'

'Of course.'

He lied to her about his wife. She knew he was married. Everyone knew. She wanted to ask him why he had lied but decided not to pursue the subject. It could wait.

'Am I to see you tonight?' he asked. The question surprised her for some reason. Perhaps she felt it had already been dealt with.

'Yes.'

'I'll pick you up.'

She gave him her address. He didn't know that part of London so she gave him directions which he wrote down in a small spiral notebook that he took from his inside pocket. As he wrote she noticed the book was full of figures and mathematical calculations which she did not understand. Each page seemed to be covered with them. When he ran out of blank spaces to write he merely wrote over the calculations.

'What time?'

'Nine.'

'O.K.'

She wanted to ask him where they were going or what they were going to do. She wanted to ask him what she should wear or whether he would like her to cook for him. She wanted to know whether he intended to fuck her but she felt she could not ask any of these things.

As he helped her into her coat he brushed her hair lightly with the back of his hand.

'You have beautiful hair.' It was the first reference

he had made to her appearance. She did not reply. For a moment his face smiled and she thought his eyes smiled too.

They walked back to the office. In the lift he said nothing and merely nodded when she got out at her floor. As she walked to her desk she remembered that she had made no attempt to pay for the meal, despite it being her invitation. He had asked for the bill and he had paid it, leaving no room for her to make a show of paying or at least offering to pay. In a other situation she would have worried and determined to bring the matter up on the next available occasion. In this situation she knew she would never mention it again.

The afternoon passed. She worked and to her surprise thought little about what had been said over lunch. She did not want to, yet. In some way she felt quietly in control and being in control meant that she did not need to speculate on the implications of remarks he had made. She had got exactly what she had wanted that Monday. It had worked exactly as she had hoped.

3

Stephanie lived in a Victorian terraced house that had been converted into flats. She had the ground floor flat which had a small garden. The flat was an expression of her personality, a quite deliberate attempt to impose herself on something tangible. It was *hers* in every sense. When her mother had died and left her a capital sum she had used it all to buy the flat. That was five years ago and now she had everything exactly as she wanted it. It was neat and clean. It was open and bright. The books, of which there were many, were all neatly sorted into subject, not size, and stacked in functional bookcases. The records were also kept in order, divided into groups and sub-groups, baroque, classical romantic, rock, jazz, male vocal, female vocal, MoR, and even a section for the one or two Christmas records she had — strictly to be played only during the weeks immediately prior to the event.

She loved the bathroom. She had spent more on that room than any other. It was large and spacious and the addition of mirrors and dark brown cork, of hanging plants and endless good-quality towels made it feel luxurious. She had so much space in the room that she had put in two chairs, comfortable armchairs. To date she had never used them.

It was half-past six. She went straight to the bathroom, only pausing to pour herself a vodka and tonic. She sat in one of the armchairs and sipped her drink as her bath ran. She looked at the room from this new angle for some minutes. She put her drink on the floor and stretched out in the chair. The steam rising from the bath and the noise of the cascading water were soporific. The alcohol warmed her too.

In the corner she had installed a wooden clothes valet. She slipped her skirt and blouse off and hung them on the valet. In her white slip she went over to the bath and turned the water off. Then she remembered George.

Somehow the two threads in her mind had not come together. She had fantasised about what her decision to approach Martin would mean. Now fantasy had become reality. Martin was coming to take her out, take her away just as she'd wanted. On the other hand she arranged her insurance — is that why she'd done it? — and George was arriving to take her out to the theatre.

His phone rang twice.

'Darling,' she tried to sound weary despite the warm feeling that elation and vodka had spread through the pit of her stomach. 'I'm going to have to stay in bed. I feel terrible. Some bug or other. I just want to crawl into bed.'

Could he help, could he bring her something round? Could he come round with stale chocolates from the Pakistani grocers on the corner, make her a cup of hot chocolate studded with floating undissolved chocolate powder and slimy milk skin because he hadn't stirred it enough or at all — George did not consider the kitchen his province — and then suggest he joined her in bed where he would fuck her, telling her it was just what she really needed to make her feel better?

'No George. I'll ring you in the morning. I'm so tired.'

She put the phone down without saying goodbye. There was something final, she felt, about ending telephone conversations without a goodbye — as though saying goodbye was a pledge against saying hello again. The lack of goodbye left an awkward question hanging in the air.

Back in the bathroom she took off her slip. Her long hair was draped over her shoulders as she tested the temperature of the water. Too hot. She ran a little cold. She added bath salts. Like mixing a cauldron. A cauldron of desire. The salts dissolved as she watched, the colouring twisting away from the crystals in irregular spirals like the smoke from discarded cigarettes. She took the rest of her clothes off. Remembering her drink she sat naked in the chair again and sipped at the vodka. The coldness of the glass in her hand made her shiver slightly. She pressed it gently against her nipple and watched as the small brown button puckered from inside her breast. She felt it tighten and stretch. The other nipple seemed to respond too, though not so quickly.

Putting her drink down again, she used the tips of her fingers that had held the glass to touch both nipples in turn, squeezing them between her fingers, rolling them between her fingers, stroking them with her middle finger. She watched what she was doing intently. She made no attempt to use the other hand.

Both nipples were firm and hard now, the puckered flesh standing out from her firm full breasts. Putting her arm across her chest, flattening her breasts against her chest, she got up and stood by the bath. The salts had dissolved completely. She stepped in, releasing her breasts to float in the water as she sunk back up to her neck.

Almost casually, as if it were an experiment, she ran her fingertip between her legs to see if she were moist, to see if her nipples had sent out any messages of sexual alert. They had not, her vagina was dry. Another experiment fails. No, another experiment is successful in proving there seems to be no correlation between the stimulation of the nipples and the production of vagina juices. Bartholin's gland holds its secrets still. On the other hand, surrounded by water, as it was, the subtle moisture of her body may simply have been washed away.

How strange, she thought, that it was quite possible for a man, or a woman, or her own hands, to perform the most careful, most thoughtful, most exciting rituals and yet if circumstances did not permit, however exciting the circumstances might ostensibly be, if *her* circumstances did not permit or want to permit, then she would feel no arousal, and little desire. It wasn't the same for men, or it didn't appear to be. Not in her experience at least. Everyman. Every ready. (Unless, of course, he had a problem. But that was not in ordinary circumstances.)

She remembered dancing in a man's arms when she was very young and feeling the snake of his penis uncurl against her navel. She knew exactly what it was, and it did not repulse her or excite her: it just seemed to her entirely curious that a man should lack control of such a major part of his anatomy. But of course, she lacked control too. When she had been taken by that boy up into a darkened room in his house, while his parents watched television downstairs, when he had pulled her knickers aside and thrust two fingers deep inside her, she had had no control of the liquid heat he found inside her, she had had no control of the mounting passion she had felt as his fingers drove up and down inside her until she almost screamed with pleasure. The first time she had been penetrated, pricked, prodded, poked. The first time she had felt live, greedy, fat fingers squirming up into her, mauling her, prying into her, impaling her, pushing at her soft silky wet cunt.

The thought of that heat, so intense and pure, had aroused her now. She did not need her finger to test her vagina this time. It would be wet. No subtlety for the water to hide.

She thought of Martin. She thought of the sound of his voice and his eyes and his mouth. She wanted to associate her arousal with her picture of him. Her mind flicked deliberately between the memory of the physical sensations in the darkened room and the memory of his eyes as he looked unblinkingly into hers.

She made no attempt to touch her body now, and left her arms resting along the sides of the bath, her fingertips hanging down into the warm water. She felt no urgency, no need to propel her body to any kind of fulfilment. It was enough to drift in and out of her feeling of passion: to keep it at arm's length, neither allowing it to overwhelm her or to dissipate. Her mind wandered on to other things, the small patch on the ceiling where the wallpaper had come unglued, whether she wanted another drink, how rude that woman at the station had been pushing her way on to the train in front of all the other people who had been waiting. But then she would pull herself back and feel that boy's chubby fingers pressed into her vagina, feel his mouth on hers, his uncertainty as he pushed his tongue between her lips. Feel the studded choking climax as she clung to him, praying he would not take his fingers away too soon as another part of her could hear the laughter and applause from the television in the room below. Then her arousal would return and with it she would think of Martin again.

As if to test her own self-awareness she dipped her finger down between her thighs, watching the water ripple as she moved her legs apart. Her clitoris was dry, dried out by the water, and the lips of her vagina sealed. With her middle finger she forced her way through to find her sheath as liquid as she had expected. The wetness was silky, oily, and hot. When she was at school she had put her fingers in a bowl of mercury and had never forgotten the peculiar feel of the liquid substance which left her hand quite dry. This was the same wetness, quicksilver wetness.

Martin would be circumcised. She made no attempt to remove her hand and no attempt to move it. His penis would have the cleanliness of a surgeon's hands, scrubbed and pink, and he would be circumcised. His pubic hair would be black and very wiry and coarse. It would scratch against her skin, it would chaff her skin. Strands of hair would get caught in her thick pubic hair. He would lie, his head resting against her thigh, and pick the trapped hairs out, counting them as he did so.

Almost unconsciously, her hand was moving between her legs and probing upwards as if to test the depth of her excitement. For a moment she allowed herself to feel the pleasant sensation of her fingers stroking her clitoris, and then, it called for no sacrifice or thought, she stopped.

She did not want to think of what he had said at lunch time. She did not want to dwell on what he had said or even to remember what he had said besides the amount necessary to remember out of considerations of politeness. Obviously she did not want to ask questions to which he had already given the answers. But beyond that she would not allow herself to go. No speculation on his motives, his reasons, his abilities, his attitudes, his lie. It was quite pointless, like schoolgirls gathering for an illicit cigarette and asking the endless unanswerable questions about whether and when and who and what some macho cowboy would or would not do, had or had not done, in reality or imagination.

No speculation. The facts were good enough. He had taken her to lunch. He had invited her to see him that evening. No speculation.

The water was getting cold. She ran in a little more hot and took up the soap and sponge. Purposefully she washed herself and stood up to get out of the bath. Water ran off her body. Small rivulets were caught in her thick pubic hair to form a stream cascading off the matted hairs between her legs. It looked like she was peeing.

Nor would she allow herself endless hours, she had two more hours, of decision as to clothes. It didn't matter. She would wear something pretty, but whatever came to hand. The indulgence of outfitting herself in front of the mirror, discarding this, rejecting that, trying on the gamut of her wardrobe, was too silly for this evening, this occasion. For some reason it was more important to feel adult, to feel in control. She was an adult.

With deliberate casualness she began to dress. She had decided that she must wear matching underwear, which limited her choice to a rather greying white set or the newer beige that she had bought on impulse and seldom worn. All her other underwear was mixtures of this and that, panties bought here, bra, slips, vests from anywhere, wherever the necessity arose. In fact, the beige was the only possible choice. That decision had only taken a minute or two, so her resolve was holding.

And it held. She dressed quickly now. Black skirt and cream silk blouse — admittedly her best. And her best black leather belt. It was too warm for tights. Sensible shoes. She allowed herself a brief debate and settled for the tighter, higher heeled black shoes — but not the highest.

It was eight. The slight euphoria the vodka had created was gone. She sat on the sofa and watched the door apprehensively. After ten minutes she decided that was unproductive. What else could she do? There was nothing else. Nothing else she cared to do but sit and wait. She closed her eyes and rested her head on the back of the chair.

The memory game was what she needed now. She had a game she played with herself to try to remember some incident precisely, in the minutest possible detail: every colour, taste, smell, feeling. The odd thing was that it would take only a minute or two before the flow of accurate minutiae gave way to a reverie of quite different details. Details of emotions, details of perceptions, details of what she had once been.

That was the distraction she needed now to pass an awkward hour. Something she had not thought of recently. Begin. It was five years ago. He was called James. Older than her. Begin with the details. Begin with the way he didn't bother to open the car door for her. Or wait for her. He just went straight to his front door, opened it with his key, and stood waiting. Nor had he bothered to offer her drink or coffee or anything. When she was inside he had closed the door and led the way upstairs. She remembered exactly what he said. 'It's up here.' She remembered she had thought that since he was obviously referring to sex perhaps the 'it' was his genitals, kept somewhere at the top of the stairs in a storage jar of formaldehyde until needed. She remembered all the details. The carpet was red. He was wearing corduroy trousers and a V-necked sweater and rather old suede shoes with frayed laces. The bedroom had a cream counterpane and curtains with a pattering of tiny flowers. As she took off her clothes she remembered the alarm clock had cartoon characters on the face. Mickey Mouse, Goofy. One of its legs had broken off and it was supported by a slim paperback, perhaps a little too slim because the clock was not quite level. It also had a very loud tick.

His name was James but everyone called him Jim. Jim. He was twenty-four with dark brown hair and brown eyes. When he took his clothes off he had a scar on his shin and no hair on his body except around his penis. This hair was long, the longest she had seen, but there wasn't much of it. His stomach was flat, almost concave, and the flesh across it creased and wrinkled when he sat down. What else? An old house but not Victorian, with an odd smell, not polish or food or damp or sweat. A smell of its own. She was wearing a green skirt and a green patterned sweater and boots. It was winter and cold. Jim had put on a gas fire which hissed and spluttered before it turned to glowing red. He had kissed her as she stood warming herself by it and she could remember the back of her calves getting hot through her tights. When she took her tights off there were blotchy red marks on her legs.

The room was soon warm. Warm enough to lie naked on top of the blankets, rather old blankets trimmed in satin blue edging. She was not naked to begin with though he had taken all his clothes off straight away. She had kept her knickers on. She was not in the least shy. Now she couldn't remember why she had kept them on but she did remember clearly that she had not bothered to take them off until they were wet from her juices. Jim had fingered her clitoris and the lips of her cunt until she felt every inch of her sex was soaking, running with the saliva of sex. Then he had stopped touching her altogether and without saying a word she got up and took her knickers off standing naked, her legs open so he could see her nether lips as he lay beneath her on the bed.

Jim's prick was large and erect. She bent down and took it in one hand so it stood absolutely upright. She knelt on the bed beside him and then moved so that her thighs were astride his. Then she lowered herself on to his penis, only releasing her hand when it was firmly home and deeply imbedded inside her. She reached up to just under her navel and prodded her stomach.

'I can feel it here,' she told him.

She lent back and ground her cunt down on to his penis, her pubic hair pushing against the long wisps of his. He moved little. It was not required. She moved little and came. She did not remember making any kind of noise but he told her that she had shouted out, almost screamed, as she came.

After her orgasm she had wanted him to come like that with her on top but in the end he had taken her on her back. She had not felt him come. After being on top, having him so deeply inside her, this position gave her only the mildest sensations. But he had come.

She had not wanted to go home, but for some reason she felt she should. She didn't want him to think of her as conventional, demanding love, cuddles, reassurance as the price of sex. She wanted him to think of her as brave, wanton, careless. Modern . . .

The memory ended there. There was no more. James was only that incident. He had made no other impact on her life. His memory was only material for masturbation or distraction. Perhaps they were the same thing.

It was five past nine when she opened her eyes. The wonder of it being later than nine made her smile with pleasure until it occurred to her that Martin might be late, that she might have even more time to kill.

4

She had been watching television when the doorbell rang. It was nine-twenty. As calmly as she could she turned off the set and walked to the door avoiding the temptation to look in the mirror one final time. He was dressed in jeans and sweater. She had never seen him in anything casual before, only ties and suits.

'Good evening,' she said with a grin.

'Hello.'

'Come in.'

He walked past her into the room.

'Would you like a drink?'

'Look, I'm sorry, I can't stay.'

She turned to look at him. In his eyes she could see something she could not understand. Perhaps it was guilt, perhaps desire.

'You'll have a drink?' she said, trying to keep her voice light and humorous. 'Scotch?'

He took the glass from her, refusing water or soda or ice. 'You know I'm married.' He was nervous, tense.

'Yes.'

'Doesn't it make a difference?'

'To what?'

'I don't know why I didn't tell you at lunch.'

'I knew you were married. I know where you live. I don't know your wife or what her name is or what she does for a living and I don't want to know.'

'And what do you want?'

Surely she had told him over lunch, at least implied it. What had they talked about.

'I want you to take me to bed.'

'So I gather.'

'Don't be smug.'

'Aren't I allowed to be a little smug? It's not every day that an attractive woman asks me to screw her.'

He had used the word deliberately to see if it had any effect on her. It had none. She sat opposite him, swirling the drink in her hand and making the Scotch climb the sides of her glass, watching as its viscosity left an arched trail on the inner surface and then seeing if she could get the Scotch higher still on the next pass.

'You said you couldn't stay.'

'Not for long. I'm sorry. I thought I'd be able to get away for longer.'

'From your wife?'

'Yes. Do you want me to go now?'

'I was going to ask at lunch why you bothered to lie.'

'But you didn't.'

'No.'

'Why not?'

'I suppose because I didn't want to know.'

'I'm afraid this is not a situation I've been in before.'

He was not looking at her when he said it and she wondered why he felt the need to lie again. It was hardly necessary.

'Neither have I.' That was not a lie.

She knew that there was nothing else to say. She knew that now the bridge between word and deed had to be crossed however faultingly, however clumsily. Physical contact.

Stephanie stood up, put her drink down, and walked over to where he was sitting. She bent from the waist as elegantly as possible, ignoring the puzzled look on his face, and kissed him. (The rest was up to him.) She did not open her mouth, wanting to save the moment when she felt the hot warmth of his tongue push into her mouth, as she would save the moment when his penis first entered her body. Then, his tongue trying to prise a way into her mouth, she allowed entry — as though being forced.

She straightened up and walked away to pour him another drink. On the floor by his chair was a rather battered rug. She laid her drink beside it and knelt on the rug, stretching out to take his hands. For a moment her mouth was level with his crotch and she kissed the material where she thought his penis might be. Then he knelt too and they kissed again. This time she allowed his tongue to enter immediately — the hymen of her mouth broken by their first kiss.

As the kiss continued she eased herself down on to the floor trying to take him with her without breaking the kiss. It was impossible to accomplish the move with any grace and still remain coupled: perhaps it was possible for subtle dancers' bodies, a modern ballet, but for ordinary mortals support had to be given in awkward graceless jerks. Both minds trying to dream their way from kneeling to lying: trying to imagine the formless ballet.

Martin broke the kiss first and moved down to kiss her neck. He kissed between the folds of material of her blouse, where the skin was taut against bone, where he could see the rise of her breasts under the silk. He cupped her left breast in his hand, not caressing it but merely feeling its depth and weight. She felt his penis swell slightly at this first real intimacy.

His hand was a provocation. She rolled on top of him, forcing his head up again as she sought his mouth to kiss. She pushed her tongue deep into his mouth while she pressed her body to his. Taking both his hands by the wrists she moved them so that they were pinned above his head. She could feel his erection now, like an iron rod between their bodies. Still holding his hands she wriggled her body against his, trying to create the maximum friction against his penis. She took her mouth away from his and made the movements of her groin more deliberate. He was smiling. She realised she was grinding her teeth.

He tried to move his hands. For a moment she resisted, but only for a moment. After all, he did not understand the game. His hands moved to her waist, pulling her blouse out of the back of her skirt, moving to unclip her bra. As he pulled the hooks from the eyes he moved his mouth to kiss her breasts, first through the silk and then, as his hands worked on the buttons and he moved the material aside, he kissed her flesh. At first he avoided her nipples, kissing instead all around the ample flesh, then he finally sunk his mouth, perhaps even his teeth, into the pluckered tight skin at the centre. After a moment he methodically dealt with the other breast in the same way. Then he stopped and sat up.

Making no attempt to cover her breasts, she handed him his drink. Tableau of secret lovers, lunchtime lovers, never time to undress. Or teenagers on the rug in the front room hoping no one would think to come in. Except there was time and they were not teenagers. Almost absent-mindedly, she moved her hand on to his crooked knee. She clasped it tightly then dropped her hand into his lap and clasped his penis. It was still iron-hard. He made no attempt to speak or drink. He looked straight into her eyes.

She stood up and walked into the bedroom without looking back. She had managed to get up gracefully. She had managed not to look back. Nor did she close the door or particularly aim to stand where he could get tantalising glimpses of her as she undressed. But without moving, she saw that he could glimpse her through the open door as she shed her clothes. She saw him watch as she stooped to take her knickers from around her ankles, the long slit of her sex displayed, stretched, the labia like the wrinkled gills of mushroom.

She climbed on to the bed out of his view and turned on the bedside light. Her heart was beating rapidly, her cunt was wet. As she lay on her back she imagined she could feel a dampness between her buttocks. Surely her wetness was not seeping out. Now she could not see him she had to depend on listening for him. At the moment there was no sound. He hadn't moved. Perhaps a slight clink of the ice in his glass: no, the ice must have melted by now; it must be some other noise. He hadn't moved.

For a moment nothing happened. She drew her knees up slightly towards her chest, her legs bent and open. She lay naked on her bed and felt naked. He sat fully clothed on her rug. Was he feeling a smug male anticipatory pleasure? The implications of the moment waited in the wings for action to bring them on stage: for implication to become consequence.

He got up. From the bed she heard him moving. She heard the kitchen door open and the tap running and then stop. She could not hear him drink. Another silence. Then footsteps and he stood before her.

He did not wait for any significant exchange of looks

between them, any narrowing of eyes, any widening of eyes. He glanced at her briefly and then concentrated on unbuttoning his shirt. Seven buttons, the last requiring him to pull his shirt from his trousers. He sat on the bed and removed his shoes and socks. She smiled to herself. Obviously he'd read the articles on how to undress in front of your lover: never stand in nothing but your socks. Standing again he took off his trousers. She moved slightly, unconsciously, some unknown impulse moving her body slightly to one side.

Again as he drew his pants away from his penis he did not pause. No announcement, signalled with an intense stare, that the moment of revelation had arrived. He merely slipped his pants to the floor and came round the bed to lay besides her. His penis was flaccid again. (He was circumcised – mental note of congratulation to the lucky lady.) From lying on her back she turned on to her side. Her nipples brushed his chest. She thought she could feel the tip of his prick against her thigh but wasn't sure. She kissed him lightly and smiled. She kissed him again. His arm had moved under her until his hand was behind her head and he could pull her mouth on to his, push his tongue into her and feel hers competing for the dominance of penetration.

His erection grew rapidly. She felt it pushing against her belly as their bodies collided. It was hot. Often she had thought of it like a third person pushing up for air as it was crushed in the first clinches of sex: it always seemed curiously disconnected, curiously redundant and out of place until it was in place, until it was connected. That thought, the thought of his penis pushing into her, seized her quite sharply and she had to catch her breath. Suddenly it was happening, Martin was happening. He was in her bed, fucking her or about to. He was naked. She was naked. She was wet and open and wanted the hot penis, the hot penis pressing against her navel inside her. And then she would know she had made dreams come true.

He didn't touch her nipples. He didn't touch her clitoris or push his fingers into her cunt. He just kissed her and let her feel his erection. His hand rested in the small of her back allowing him to increase the pressure on his penis by pressing her into it. She could feel the little pool of wet his penis was producing.

With only the smallest movement, still facing each other on their side, his penis was inside her. Just inside her. She could feel the rim of his penis against the lips of her cunt. In this position it could not penetrate any further. Nor had it need. He was rubbing it slowly in and out of her and she was coming. She was coming and wanting to come and not wanting to come and trying to stop herself from coming all at the same time, just on the delicate movement of one inch of his hot penis. His penis burned with heat; she had never felt such heat. She pulled her mouth away from his to allow herself the pleasure of gasping for air and moaning in ecstasy and she came. She came hotly, intensely, exquisitely. An orgasm that matched the way it had arrived, hot, short and with very little underlying sensation. It was over almost as soon as it had begun.

In an almost magical way she found she was lying on her back and his penis was buried deep inside her as he looked down on her. She could not remember the movement. She could not remember feeling his prick slide up into her. It was there. Just there. Her hands clutched at his buttocks, pulling him further into her, but he was as deep as he could go.

He did not move. He did not take up a rhythm inside

her. Stephanie suddenly felt strangely disorientated. It felt as though her sexuality was draining away from her like water from a bath. She tried to search for something. She searched her erotic memories looking for some connection between this act and her sexual feelings, some connection to bring her back to reality. She flicked through the images like index cards. This man, this penis, this body, this penetration, any penetration, her orgasm, her breasts pressed into his chest, her clitoris pressed into his groin, her legs opened for him. The boy's chubby fingers inside her liquid cunt.

He started to move, his buttocks rising under her hands. She grasped them to stop him but he took this as a sign to penetrate again and he drove into her and out again. And in and out again. She was angry. She was angry with herself at not feeling the right feelings: she was angry at him for not making her feel the right feelings. She was angry. She took her hands from his buttocks.

'Don't,' she said. 'Stop.

'I want you.'

'Not like this.'

'How then?'

'Stop.'

He stopped and slowly withdrew. He lay on his back, his penis sticking out from his body glistening with her juices. He did not appear to be cross or hurt or have any emotion. He just lay there erect. She tried to concentrate on the right memory. There was a memory or perhaps it was emotion. An emotion she had felt fleetingly earlier on. He smiled at her, seemingly unconcerned, seemingly quite confident that he had not been rejected. An emotion? Something she had read?

She took his penis in one hand, curling her fingers

around the shaft, watching it swell slightly as she squeezed, watching his face as she squeezed. He smiled on. Still holding his penis in one hand she knelt beside him. It was an emotion. She could feel it pulling at her heart beat, she could feel it opening her cunt. Now she opened her legs and knelt above his penis. She eased herself down on to his penis, all the way down on to it, releasing it with her hand to hold it firmly with her cunt. She squeezed it with her cunt. She managed to envelope it further. Her disorientation had disappeared. She found his hands with hers and laced his fingers into hers, each paired finger a knot. She held his hands as she held his penis; for a moment she pressed the back of his hands into her breasts rubbing them slightly so he could see her breasts shake and her nipples tighten again.

They kissed, her tongue penetrating his mouth. She held his hands high above his head, stretching herself forward to hold them out as far as she could. And then she moved herself on his penis, pulling it out, pushing it back, squirming her clitoris against his pubic bone, riding his penis. Her first climax came almost immediately but she knew it was only the first. She rode him and did not pause for the climax to come or pass.

He tried to move his hands, unlace his fingers, but his fingers and hand were held tight. She supposed he could overcome her. She supposed he could force her over on to her back, on to his terms, but she was strong and anyway it didn't matter. It was what she thought that mattered. The emotion. Her movements were less frantic now, more purposeful, she was taking more time over each stroke, pressing down harder and grinding her clitoris into his pubic hair; pulling away and teasingly holding him at the outermost point of her cunt before allowing him back into her.

'You're making me come.'
'I know.'
'Do you want me to come now?'
'No, I want you to go on.' Then she laughed. 'Come, just come.'

She increased her rhythm again. She felt his excitement grow. She made no effort to relax her grip on his hands, in fact she tried to hold them tighter still. She could feel the heat his penis was generating inside her and her pleasure was greater than she could remember ever before. As she felt the waves of another orgasm break on the shores of her body, on her clitoris, in the small of her back, in her nipples, and then with the final intensity behind her eyes, she saw his outstretched arms and the white knuckles of her hands as she held him down.

He was coming, she could feel his prick tense ready to spit into her. She raised herself off him and held him there at the lips of her cunt. For a moment his eyes opened and he looked alarmed as she made no effort to push him back inside her. She wanted to reassure him, wanted to tell him not to worry, she would let him have his place, let him find his place. But she didn't. Instead she looked at him and said nothing. He bucked upwards but she moved up to keep his penis at bay. He tried to move his hands but she tightened her grip. She only wanted to hear him say please. *Please*. The idea caught her like a fire. That was precisely what she wanted. *Say please, you bastard. Say please may I. Please can I. Please will you let me*. She drove herself down on to him and released his hands. He pushed into her cunt and came instantly, flooding her, filling her, pumping into her.

He slackened almost immediately. With her kneeling

over him his penis slid out of her very quickly after he'd come and as she moved off him she could feel how wet she was. She'd read in one of the books that you should scoop the sperm out of your cunt and lick it off your fingers. Great blobs of white sperm like runny ice cream. She had read that if you took the wet flaccid penis into your mouth it would harden again . . .

'Do you have to go?'

'Do you want me to go.'

'Don't answer a question with a question.'

'I have to go. O.K.?'

'Do you want another drink? Or coffee?'

'And a post-coital cigarette? No.'

She got up from the bed and walked, naked, into the living room to get herself a Scotch. When she got back into the bedroom she saw him looking at her body, the shapes and shadows of her body. She did not hurry across the room.

'I'm not usually so . . .' She didn't want to say aggressive.

He laughed. 'I don't particularly want to know what you are usually.'

'Not like this.'

'Does it matter?'

'I surprised myself.'

'Is that a rare event?'

'Oh yes. I very rarely do anything unpredictable. I never do anything unpredictable. Nine-to-five hours, nine-to-five life, all neatly packaged, all neatly ordered. Very little happens in my life. You are the first thing . . .'

'Really?' Was it that he didn't sound surprised or that he wasn't that interested?

'Yes. Perhaps that's why I wanted you so much.'

'And now you've had me?'

'Ah, that's the question, isn't it? Do you think I'm mistress material?'

'I didn't say I was looking for a mistress.'

'Just casual fucks?'

'If that's how you want to put it.'

'With me?'

'Yes.'

'You'd never have asked me would you?'

'Asked you what?'

'Chivalry is dead.'

'I'm a slow worker and I'm married, which is a severe handicap in trying to seduce nice girls like you.'

'Is that how you see me?'

'What?'

'A nice girl.'

'Well, you are.'

'It's not very flattering to be a nice girl.'

'You're a very beautiful nice girl.'

'I'd rather be ugly and evil.'

'No you wouldn't.'

'The perennial nice girl, nice, predictable and boring?'

'Perhaps you should use the past tense.'

5

There was very little typing to be done. There was very little of anything to be done. The seasonal slump. The sun was surprisingly warm, streaming in through the large windows all round the open-plan office making the heating feel too high. None of the double-glazed windows could be opened. The air seemed stuffy and stale, the usual clacking of typewriters reduced to an occasional burst somewhere from the other side of the room.

Stephanie wished there had been more to do. She had wanted to keep her mind occupied, keep it away from the memories of the night until they could be properly digested, time acting as the intestine of the mind. As it was she was free to dwell on what had happened, to turn it over in her mind, to rehearse the images, to run it back, to run it forward, to stop at some particular moment and replay it over and over again – a video recorder with remote control. She saw his penis, his flat naked stomach, her breasts ballooned up against him in their embrace. Like looking directly into the sun without sunglasses. The image of the blazing golden circle left burnt on the retina. Even with the eyes closed, in the black behind the eyelids, the golden circle remained. Look long enough and hard enough and the only thing ever to be seen again would be that fuzzy round golden penumbra.

Martin was somewhere in the building, somewhere up above her. She had not seen him, nor did she want to see him today. What did he see when he closed his eyes?

What she remembered most, what she felt most — because it was so recent she could feel it as well as see it in her mind — what was left burning behind her eyes, was kneeling on him, taking his hands, pushing down on to his penis, encasing it in her, trapping it, holding it and using it. Being on Martin. Holding him. Holding him down.

Her response to him? Kneeling above him holding his hard hot penis tightly in her fist. Moving her cunt over it until she found the opening and pushed down and down on to him. Felt him ride into her, fill her until he would go no further, until he struck home, a bar of iron buried almost vertically inside her.

She caught herself shifting in her chair. She was actually squirming, moving her bottom to and fro, unconsciously trying to reseat herself, unconsciously looking for his penis with her cunt, hoping it might be here, growing out of her typing chair to be conveniently fucked again. She looked round in case anyone had been watching what to her was a blatantly sexual act. No one had.

Of course the memory was wrong. The memory was wrong. She hadn't used her hands! Both her hands held his above his head. She had wanted to hold his penis and guide him into her but she could not, because she also wanted to hold his hands down, stop him, pin him there.

She knew exactly what she wanted to do to him. She

could see it, feel it, every movement, every act Stephanie could imagine. So real.

She would kneel at the side of his chest as Martin lay on the bed and slip a silk sleeping mask over his eyes making sure it fitted snugly over the bridge of his nose. She did not want him to see anything. The cords would be white and silky. Tie his feet, first looping the cord twice around each ankle and then securing it to the leg of the bed at each corner. The procedure would be the same with his wrists except that she would not need to use the legs of the bed as the headboard had metal corner posts sturdy enough to take the bonds. She'd tie his wrists tightly. She did not want him to be able to escape. Good knots too, from Girl Guide training. She had the badge still, somewhere.

He would be naked and erect now, his penis like a tent pole of a marquee awaiting the canvas. She would be fully clothed. Without taking off her shoes she'd pull down her white knickers and, careful not to snag them in the high heels, step out of them. Still warm from her, she'd pick them up and throw them on to his chest. Pulling her skirt up she'd straddle his penis, reach behind her to hold his penis in her fist – now she had her hands free – then squeeze it and squeeze it moving her cunt back until she could feel him at the bottom of her vagina and feel her wetness spread on to him as she pushed him home deep into her. When he was in, deep in, she'd let her skirt fall back around her, rearrange it daintily, careful that it was not creased. His cock hidden.

During all this time Martin would not say anything or try to move. He would obey. An obedient object.

The first book she had bought had a chapter on bondage. She read it with no particular interest, but perhaps it made a deeper impression on her than she imagined. Perhaps it was this that was conditioning her response. Pornography makes puppets of us all. Puppets dancing to the same tunes. The same tunes repeated over and over again. Black stockings and suspenders, large full breasts, tiny G-string knickers, huge Negroid phalluses, flexed-muscled chests. Like advertising jingles never to be forgotten — 'I wonder where the yellow went . . .'

And like advertising there was the need to find new more exciting images, the need to do something different, something original, something to catch the eye — or in the case of pornography the sexual imagination — before it thinks of something original for itself.

It had occurred to her that what was described as sexual perversion was precisely that — the product of pornography's attempt not to bore its audience. Except there was the question of which came first. Did pornography write about sadism before sadism existed or did they write about it because sadism was a theme of actual sex life? She had to admit the latter was probably the answer, in which case, in her own position, her fantasies came from something other than the rather graphic reading material she was indulging in. Well, at least in part.

It was not a good book. The commentary linking the examples supposedly taken from hard-core pornography was dull and patronising. It was fond of quoting Krafft-Ebing and Havelock Ellis as though their explanation ended all discussion. Scientific fact. It was fond of pointing out grammatical errors in the writing and obvious mistakes where the author of an extract had forgotten that human beings are limited to one pair of hands and given his victim, or inquisitor, though more usually the victim, an extra hand or two during a particularly purple passage. Presumably the writer had been carried away with passion along with his creations. The commentary was boring but the examples were not. The examples were astonishing. Astonishing. She had never read or thought such things. Astonishing because, however small the mass, reading must be a mass activity so these things must be common, must be known, must be recognised by a mass.

The image of Christ on the cross was an image of sado-masochism and bondage.

The golden stream. A man lay under the golden stream bound hand and foot.

The stockings were silk and the palest grey. She wore a silk grey suspender belt to support them but otherwise was naked. Under the top of the stocking, on the inside of the thigh, a red rose was crushed. The thorn of the rose had drawn blood.

You will be caned with your knickers drawn tightly between your legs. You will be caned again with your knickers taken completely off. You will be caned grasping your ankles firmly with your hands and then you will be caned lying across the arm of the chaise longue.

You will drink the golden stream and be glad you are allowed to drink.

She made him wear her shoes. They were much too small for him but he dare not argue with her so he undressed completely, she had ordered this too, and put on her high-heeled shoes. She made him walk around in front of the women . . .

The range seemed endless and yet peculiarly limited. Anything that could be done with an eight-inch sword of flesh and a slightly larger and elasticated receptacle; anything the sword could be driven into or the receptacle receive. Any number of swords, any number of receptacles; numbered combinations, two to the right, three to the left. Any fraction of a degree, from sadism short of amputation to masochism short of suicide. But all sharing the same end. The short ejaculation of sperm. In cunt, hand, mouth, wine glass; over navels, knickers, leather corsets, rubber sheets. The whole complex lengthy fantasy culminating in three seconds of ejaculation.

Usually the ejaculation triggered female orgasm too. But it was very much an afterthought. This book, like the others, was aimed at the male market. It did not imagine female readers — except in its own fantasy world — and did not cater for them, whatever catering might mean. Females were brought to orgasm only in strict relation to the male. Even the lesbian scenes were clearly intended for the titillation of the male: and the male was present *in absentia* even as the women wielded huge penis-shaped dildoes.

In fact the author, who used a woman's name, dismissed the idea that females could be stimulated visually or that females would get any sexual pleasure from reading pornography or looking at pornographic photographs. That was the male province — or prerogative? Women were more subtle creatures. For women sex was a means to an end, the production of children. Women carried the torch of reproduction that carried mankind forward. For them sex was serious, not frivolous or fantastic. Of course, women could be objects, sex objects. Could be used, abused. But at the service of man and man's fantasies, not their own.

The image of Christ on the cross was an image of sado-masochism and bondage. No wonder it lasted so long.

Someone said the difference between man and animals was the ability to fantasise. Well, she had a fantasy. The writer was wrong. She had a fantasy. Her secret. Every bit as crude as a male fantasy, every bit as stimulating, and frivolous. With man as the object. For her the only question, a question she could play with, take out and play with in the watches of the night, was whether she wanted to make it come true.

6

Stephanie wanted to wait for Martin to come to her. She didn't see him for three days; he was in the building but they did not meet even accidentally. When they did it was he who came over to her desk.

'My wife's out on Tuesday.'
'Is that an invitation?'
'I could pick you up.'
'Why don't I come round to you?'
She watched the hesitation and the slight tightening of the muscles around his eyes.
'Is she away for long?' she asked, giving him time to understand the implications.
'Two days.'
'Then I could come over?'
'Yes. Yes,' said. The second 'yes' was more affirmative.
'Good.'
'Do you know the address?'
'Yes. What time?'
'About eight.'
'Fine.'

As she watched him walk away she smiled broadly. This plan had not been in her box of delights but it was extraordinary that it made her feel so pleased with herself. Why? At his discomfiture? Because she knew it would make him acutely uncomfortable having her in his marital home? Because she could deliberately misbehave? Because she would enjoy behaving badly, doing what she had never dared to do? Her smile was firmly set.

Late-night shopping meant the shops were open when she left the office. In no particular hurry she browsed through the windows until, on impulse, she went into a shoe shop to try the black court shoes that had caught her eye. The size was perfect and she bought them without hesitation.

At home she tried them on again, wheeling around in front of the mirror in the bathroom. They made her look taller. She took them off carefully and put them away before undressing and running her bath.

George was late. Ten minutes late. George was invariably ten minutes late. She had dressed carelessly in old comfortable clothes. She had hardly bothered with make-up. George no longer merited attention to her appearance. She knew she would have to tell him soon that he hardly merited her attention at all, but she did not plan to do that tonight. She wanted him for experimental purposes tonight, after which he might well find her welcome unaccountably withdrawn.

Her plan required she be civil to him. At least civil. She could not stand the thought of another Japanese dinner however. The thought of little Oriental women bowing and smiling and fetching hot towels did not suit her mood at all. They went to the local Italian at her insistence. Of course, George didn't mind at all. His pleasure. To the strains of highlights from Verdi, a seemingly short tape played on a loop over and over again, she listened as George told her the sort of day he'd had. The buying and selling, the coming and going, the ups and downs: what was said over pints in the foggy bar of a city pub, what the man from Manchester said, after they'd plied him with Scotch, about the man from Bolton who was actually his boss. Pausing only to eat, to drink, to call the waiter, to ask her if the food was all right. Pausing only to ask for the bill, George lectured on until they were back in his flat. She'd wanted it to be his flat.

His flat was modern, functional and unattractive. No personality, no attempt to change it from what it was when he moved in. Only furniture that was necessary — bed, wardrobe, sofa, chair, table. A cooker that was used only for making toast, covered with breadcrumbs as it had never been cleaned. A carpet in a colour so neutral it was impossible to tell what colour it had once been described as. Two or three pictures badly positioned and obviously bought with no thought. She had always suspected they covered some dirty stain, so uncharacteristic were they.

George offered to make coffee but she refused it. He poured them brandy. She had drunk wine with her meal but she didn't think that accounted for the strange fluttering feeling she was experiencing. A sort of freedom. A lack of responsibility. The freedom of not caring. She took a sip of her brandy. George was still talking sitting across from her in a William Morris loose-covered wing chair. She looked into his crotch. His legs were open and she tried to imagine how, in the folds and creases of material, his penis was curled. It always looked as though there was no room for it all, as though, like a jack-in-a-box, it only existed when freed.

Stephanie would free it. From the sofa she slid down on to the floor. She did not want to walk over to him, she wanted to crawl on all fours until her head was between his knees.

'What are you doing?' He emphasised the 'are'. At least she stopped the incessant flow of business acumen.

'Crawling to you.'

'You've never done that before. Are you all right'

The taboo of originality, sin of sins.

'Don't you want me to crawl?'

He laughed, not wholly easily. 'Like a dog?'

'Japanese women would crawl for you.'

'You're in a funny mood. What's the matter with you.'

'Does something have to be the matter?'

'No. I just thought . . .'

'What?'

'Do you want to go to bed?'

She unzipped his fly. Working her way past his Y-fronts, she found his penis curled up, tucked up out of harm's way down between his legs. She managed to pull the Y-fronts to one side enough to expose a little of the withered root to the air. She blew on it. It stirred. Just a flicker of movement. She giggled like a girl. A girl with an uncurling penis.

'Are we going then?' He meant to bed.

She blew again, then moved forward so she could lick the hairy flesh she had uncovered. The tip was still trapped under the material but as she laid saliva on the stem she could feel the blood pounding in and the penis arching out trying to free itself. She watched its efforts and then, hooking her fingers under it, she pulled it clear of the obstruction. Fully erect now, the eye winked its 'thank you' at her. She responded by taking it in her fist like the handle of some machine, the lever to be pulled to start the process. The foreskin still covered the tip which projected above the top of her hand. She kissed the foreskin and then squeezed her fist tight. She squeezed it tighter like a wrist exercise. Squeeze, release, squeeze, release. She knew he would want her to pull the foreskin back. She squeezed again.

'Hey!'

'What?' She looked up at his face, suddenly remembering he had a face, eyes, a mouth, a voice. She had been concentrating so much on his penis it had seemed a person in itself.

'Hurt.' He said it like a little boy not sure whether to complain in case playtime stopped.

She knew he wanted her to take him in her mouth. It was, after all, the thing that gave him most pleasure. She knew he regarded the act of intercourse as a very pale second best to coming in her mouth. He had made that very clear in everything but words. He moaned louder when he came, he thrust into her more strongly, he was always happier, brighter, more talkative, more considerate afterwards. Whereas she could never get over the impression that intercourse was a chore for him, something that had to be done, like investing in a savings account so that every so often one would be paid a bonus. No bonus without investment.

George hadn't touched her. He had sat there with his legs apart, his hands on the arms of the chair. Armchair sultan, not at all what she had in mind. She took his penis, the foreskin still in place, into her mouth as far back in her throat as it would go. She opened her eyes. The zip of his trousers was brass-coloured. There was a light stain on the front of his pants. She took his penis out of her mouth. She had not sucked it or licked it, just held it as though to measure some interior dimension by it.

For a moment she stopped. She could see he wanted her to go on, wanted her to pull his foreskin back and go on. In a way she had never realised the power she had in sex. The absolute power.

'Do you want to go to bed?' He sounded puzzled.

She said nothing, looking from his penis to his face and back to his penis. Constricted as it was by his pants and trousers it stood swollen and veined. She stroked it with one hand. There was no sign of his balls; they must have been caught under his trousers. It must be uncomfortable for him, she thought, though he seemed not to want to move.

It was her secret. She thought of herself impaled on Martin's prick, screwing down on his prick, holding his hands stretched and tight as she crammed him into her cunt.

'Nice.' George's voice brought her back to the room. She was still stroking him gently. Too gently to bring him off, not gently enough to allow him to soften. He wanted more. She had made him want more.

'Stand up.' He didn't look as though he wanted to.
'Bed?'
'Stand up,' she repeated.

George stood. His trousers fell away from his waist. Glimpsed under clothes like this flesh seemed unpleasant, white, fatty, unstressed, like whale blubber cut out and lying on the factory ship waiting to be melted down and made into soap, plastic, perfume. Still kneeling, she rose from her haunches until her mouth was level with his penis which was standing out from his body now, a barber's pole without the stripes, a flag pole with no flag. She kissed it lightly once or twice. He moaned but she knew it was more a moan of request than an expression of any pleasure.

She stood up. He could not keep the look of disappointment from his eyes. She delighted in it. The disappointment gave her real pleasure and made her smile. Poor man, he had really thought she was going to kneel in front of him and take him with her mouth.

'You're in a funny mood.'

'Yes.'

It was true. She felt she was in a mood, not funny, but strange. Funny peculiar. She turned and walked into the bedroom. Funny peculiar that she did not really care whether he followed her or not. He could stand there with his erection wilting away if that's what he wanted. He followed her and starting taking off his clothes. His penis had wilted. But she was naked before him. He had never learned the technique required to undress with some grace: he always took his socks off last. She lay naked on her side watching him pull his socks off without sitting down, hopping from one foot to the other. As he did his penis, now totally flaccid, flopped up and down. Finally he sat down beside her and turned to kiss her.

She allowed him to kiss her. She allowed him to finger her breasts, rub at her nipples, move his hand down to her navel at the same time turning her on to her back. She allowed him to finger her clitoris. She watched him doing it. But she could not say she felt him doing it. She had the odd twinge of sensation but not the slow crescendo of pleasure he was supposed to be inducing.

When he mounted her she lay with her eyes open, looking round the room, remembering how she had crawled over to him in the living room, remembering the tip of his hard penis at the back of her throat. Now as he laboured away at her, in and out, in and out, regular, equal, conscientious, the excitement was gone. The mood she was in was not the mood to fantasise. Not now. Not with him inside her. She did not want to think about sex at all. She wanted a reality, to perform a fantasy, to be a fantasy. To consummate the racing fantasies she had conceived. That was what she had tried to do earlier with George, until she realised it was only George and George would not do any more. He never had done. To make these fantasies come true, real, apparent, object and subject had to be the same man.

Before George, ordinary sex seemed only ordinary; now it was irrelevant. Irrelevant to the extraordinary freedom she had conceived. Freedom of herself. Freedom for herself. Freedom for herself.

Feeling nothing, she moaned. She moaned long and hard and loud. She began to rock her body, hug George's back, dig her fingers into his buttocks, moan again. Rock back and forth with his movement. Blow hot air into his ear. Try not to laugh. Try not to laugh. Moan again. She could feel him getting harder, breathing shorter. Ready to tense. Ready to push up into her and stay this time. Stay and shoot, and breathe again and call her darling and tell her how good that was and was she all right and he did have to work in the morning so he must get some sleep so should he call her a taxi or did she want to stay?

Stephanie took the taxi. She had wanted to be alone. As they drove she felt the wet crotch of her knickers. She looked at the taxi driver's head. How odd to be sitting with a strange man two feet away with your knickers soaked with another man's sperm. The twentieth century.

At home she did nothing. She didn't take off what little make-up she was wearing, clean her teeth, wash. She just threw her clothes in a pile on a chair in the bedroom and got into the bed naked. Her crotch was hot and sticky. She lay on her back with her legs slightly apart. It crossed her mind to masturbate but with some inexplicable logic the thought of George's sperm, still there inside her, put her off the idea. So she lay waiting for sleep to overtake her.

It didn't. She lay awake, her mind filling with images, words, deeds. She had always believed people didn't change much. They got older, more tolerant, mellower. They adapted to their surroundings, recovered from tragedy, found ways of living with the inevitable compromise; but through it all they remained essentially the same. She had always suspected people who claimed that they'd changed. But now . . . The change she had felt in the last few days was something that had surprised her.

She was not surprised that she had propositioned Martin. She had always felt that it was possible for her to take the initiative given the right man and the right circumstances. Why not? Men approached women all the time, why not the other way round? A simple statement of feminism. Women were equal to men. Of course, as things stood, with women approaching men the exception not the rule, it implied − or she assumed it implied to the male libido − more of a sexual encounter than a social one. But that might change in time. If exception became rule. Not that it mattered with Martin. A sexual encounter was all she had had in mind.

No, there was something deeper than that. Something she had not yet fully understood. He had somehow aroused in her a new feeling; a new sexual feeling, but not only sexual. It was based on sex, yes, but it was more fundamental than that. It was power, it was energy, it was light. It was confidence, and freedom.

Perhaps she was being too dramatic. Perhaps it was

nothing more than being truly satisfied sexually. Satisfied with no nagging feeling that there could have been more; with no feeling that she had given a performance; with no feeling that her satisfaction was, on the whole more due to her own commitment than her partner's. That is what Martin had made her feel. That at one and the same time he was totally in control of her and she was totally in control of him. A contradiction in terms but true for her.

Was it just that? She pumped up her pillow and adjusted her position slightly. Her eyes had adjusted to the dark and the room was full of shadows and shapes from the light filtering through the drawn curtains from the street lights outside. Shadows and shapes that as a child she would have formed into strange jungle plants growing at a fantastic rate to engulf the room in foliage.

Was it just her passion for this man that allowed her to contemplate going to his house, making love to him in his marital bed? She had never been bothered by going to bed with married men. She would never have become seriously involved with one, she knew *that* rule, but she had never been to their houses. Never seen their wives' things, eaten on their wives' table, slipped between their wives' sheets. Was that such a difference? Going to the marital home was just less hypocritical.

What would he do? Would he be embarrassed? Not if he'd invited her there, or at least agreed to her coming. He would be uncomfortable. She would have the upper hand. What a strange expression. Upper hand. The image of him pinned underneath flashed into her mind. Upper hand. Upper bunk. Uppermost.

It would be up to her. She would have to lead him. Lead him into her. She could not help smiling to herself at the thought. And as she caught herself doing it, she thought that here was the change. This sudden obsession with images of sex, scenarios of sex, fantasies like the original fantasies she had had of him. A fantasy that was so near the reality. So satisfying, converting fantasy into reality; it was like decorating a room to a plan. Like the plan the fantasy must be detailed, carefully drawn, capable of being fulfilled without the need for special equipment or extra helpers. She felt the edges of sleep fudging the sharpness of her thoughts.

His house was in the middle of a field of wheat — wheat ready to be harvested. She had to tread it down to make a path to his front door. When she looked back the path had gone. She didn't knock. The door opened and she was inside, sitting in the front room drinking warm gin. The front curtains, bright and flowery — huge sunflowers more like people's heads than flowers — were drawn. She sat in an armchair. She thought of sitting on the sofa but that was too obvious. Now she was sitting on the sofa, her drink still in her hand as she asked Martin to put his hand up her skirt and feel her. She was kissing him, pushing her tongue into his mouth, deeper and deeper as his fingers pushed into her cunt and he fucked her with his fingers. She was standing by the living-room door, wearing only her bra, a black wired bra which she did not really possess, naked but for the bra and the black high heels she had bought the other day. As she looked down at them she noticed they were dirty. How did they get dirty? She turned and walked upstairs, telling Martin to follow, aware of him looking up at her naked arse and the crack of her cunt as her legs parted to climb each step. On the top step she turned and sat down, parting her legs so that he walked right up into her cunt, right up, his mouth caressing her labia, his tongue pushing into her, feeling like a tiny penis. She sat on the top step. He lay on his stomach across the other steps so his mouth could press against her. The other woman just watched from the bottom of the stairs, not smiling, not scowling, just watching like a factory inspector making sure the job was being done in accordance with specifications. Was she wearing a white coat?

7

On the tube in the morning Stephanie saw a man eyeing a pretty girl wearing a T-shirt and no bra. As the T-shirt was armless and loose the girl's large, pendulous breasts were visible from the side under her arms. The man craned his head. She supposed he was trying to see the nipple. She watched him — the girl herself seemed totally unaware of his attention. What satisfaction was there in that? What satisfaction from a fleeting glimpse of shimmering flesh? A fleeting glimpse of unstrung nipple? Had it made him erect, sent blood coursing into his penis? Was the sending of blood satisfaction in itself for a man?

She smiled at the thought. Before she could see whether anything developed — his erection or an acquaintance — the train came to her station and she got off. She was in a good mood. Content with herself, happy for the time being to mark time, to catch up with what had happened to her and adjust. She was glad of the routines of work. Among the changes work was a stability she welcomed.

At her desk Stephanie surveyed her mail. There was nothing that would take her mind away. Just routine. She took the cover off the typewriter and started typing some work left over from yesterday — the second draft of a report on the efficacy of market research in relation to different groups of products. Apparently people interviewed, even cleverly interviewed with questions they might not realise were angled to avoid hostile responses, lied repeatedly if asked about soap, shampoo, car oil, leather goods, and perfume but were scrupulously honest when it came to wallpaper adhesive, baked beans, cigarettes, cars and depilatory creams.

It was lunchtime before she'd finished. When she'd applied for her job it was described as an 'executive assistant'. After six months she had realised that it was only 'executive' because she was given assignments by more than one person (all male) and only 'assistant' because one fifth of her work had nothing to do with typing. A fine use for a degree in sociology but executive assistants with degrees in sociology made advertising agencies feel secure, even complacent.

Stephanie was not ambitious, however. She had accepted her lot and the good money and the opportunity to bemoan the iniquities of the system with her friends. She worked to live and it allowed her to live as she wanted. Though she hated to admit it in such liberated days, the idea that she would marry and have children, that a man would arrive to 'take her away from all this' had always seemed to her proper and probable. Meantime . . .

She didn't eat lunch. She sat at her desk reading, though the words never formed any pattern of meaning and she didn't bother with the fiction of turning the pages. Her eyes glazed, thin glass through which she stared on to the pictures of her thoughts superimposed on the pages of the book. It was like being a man. Like being that man on the tube; like George. Getting your end away. That's what they said. Having it off. Casual unattached sex. That was what she was doing with Martin after all. Had done and wanted to do again. Using him. Feeling him. Not caring what he was, or who or where. If she thought about him she could get the same flicker of excitement the man on the tube presumably felt straining to catch his glimpse of nipple. A shiver of excitement to be translated into something real and physical, given the opportunity; an itch turning to a need. A need for immediate, urgent sex, to be satisfied in the nearest hole, toilet, doorway, office store cupboard. Unattached sex, not bothering to stoop to remove the knickers from your ankles.

What was happening to her? She had experienced casual sex before; sex in a toilet, cramped, uncomfortable, urgent and not totally unsatisfactory. Never quite able to dismiss the discomfort of the white porcelain digging into her back for the pleasure of a tongue on her clitoris, nor forget the ache in her knees as they bent to accommodate the awkward thrusts of a man determined to fuck her standing up, so urgent was the need. But she would dismiss it with Martin. If it was Martin. If she was doing it with Martin.

She realised her face was red. She was blushing and feeling hot. She was thinking about sex again. Sex again and again. What was happening to her?

The afternoon passed quickly. More work, more routine. No time to let her mind drift which was a relief to her. Stephanie did not understand why she seemed suddenly so concerned with sex. Was it just Martin? She was sexually infatuated with Martin. That was all. As simple as that. Putting the cover on her typewriter and saying her goodnights she walked to the lift. She had just missed one arriving in time to see the doors slide closed with a metallic rattle and to catch a glimpse of Martin standing perfectly bisected by the two doors. He gave no sign of recognition in the fraction of a second before the doors closed completely. She used the stairs.

At home she did nothing in particular. Washing needed doing and she did it. She watched a documentary on television about a new religious sect recruiting young people and taking them off to the Nevada desert where the rituals they performed had more to do with Busby Berkeley than Jesus Christ. George called and talked at length without listening, which was as well because her ability to respond in more than monosyllables appeared to be extremely limited. At ten she decided she was tired and went to bed. Like most women she had her own bedtime routine. It took half-an-hour before she pulled on a clean cotton nightdress and climbed into bed. She had forgotten to put the chain on the door and wearily got up to do it.

Settling down again she lay for a moment with the light on. She hadn't thought of Martin all evening. Not since seeing him in the lift. Why had he had such an effect on her? What was happening? She turned the light out.

It was Tuesday tomorrow. In an effort to understand she went to the nearest bookshop at lunch time. Making her way to a stand of books she had never looked at before, euphemistically described by the sign overhead as 'Health and Welfare', she began to work her way through books with titles like *Female Sexuality, Varieties of Sexual Response, The Female Predicament, Life, Love and Sex*. She flicked through them, looking at chapter headings, reading the beginnings of paragraphs, the ends of sentences, her eyes looking for phrases appropriate to her condition, or what she felt her condition to be. What did she feel her condition to be she wondered as she picked up a book on *The G-Spot*. The Awakening of Sexual Awareness in Pre-Middle Age Woman? Heightened Sexual Fantasy in Woman? Obsessional Sexual Aberration? Male Generated Sexual Impulse? The Male Libido in the Female?

As she browsed nothing in any of the books seemed to fit her case. Her case? A patient already. Your psychiatrist awaits. She wanted to know if there was a pattern, a syndrome, a complex. Klien's Syndrome. Clytemnestra's Complex. There would be reassurance in finding out she was merely a statistic, one of hundreds, one of thousands. Finding nothing conversely made her feel her situation wasn't real, wasn't proper, but something she had dreamt up because she spent so much time on her own. The product of an over-imaginative mind.

It was Tuesday tomorrow. She left the bookshop annoyed with herself. There was no explanation because there was nothing to explain. Her experience was lust. She had never experienced it before. Pure lust. And lust would become satiated, like greed. Like eating strawberries until you were sick to death of strawberries and never wanted to see another strawberry again. That was it. Simple.

Before she went back to the office she went to the underwear department of John Lewis. She didn't look among the racks of bras and knickers knowing exactly what she wanted. The underwear, or most of it, was divided by colour and she walked straight to the black section. She found a black camiknicker in her size and a matching suspender belt and went in the changing room to try them on. Normally she wouldn't have bothered but today she wanted to make sure they fitted so she could get used to wearing them before tomorrow.

Taking her skirt and blouse off she pulled the camiknicker over her head, bending to fasten the studs between her legs. She pressed them together against the crotch of her white cotton knickers. It fitted perfectly. Only glancing at herself quickly in the mirror she took it off again, tried the suspender belt around her waist and hurriedly dressed again. On the way to the cash desk she found a pair of charcoal grey stockings, it was years since she'd worn stockings, and she paid for the three items feeling strangely that the other customers were all watching her.

The afternoon was busy and she was able to submerge herself in work. In fact it was not until she got home and took her purchases out of their bag that any thought of tomorrow or Martin occurred to her. She made herself some coffee. It tasted stale. Must be getting towards the end of a packet. Mental note to buy more. Mental note to buy tissues and toilet paper and shampoo and washing-up liquid . . . Too much for a mental note; she wrote it down immediately in her shopping list notebook. Anything else? A leather penis restrainer in black hide with twelve steel studs.

Stephanie took the new underwear into the bedroom and got completely undressed. She did spend too much time on her own. But she'd never wanted to have a flatmate, male or female, and she'd always been able to afford not to. She had never felt it was a problem living alone. But it did allow you too much time to think. Naked she picked up the camiknicker, bit the price tag off and slipped it over her head. Now, with no cotton knickers on, she had to do up the studs between her legs against the soft flesh and hair of her labia. It seemed odd somehow, feeling the cold bright clips at her fingers and at the same time the soft warmth of flesh. Why odd? Because her awareness of her cunt was so intense now. It seemed a creature in itself, like a dog demanding attention, wanting to be fed.

Without a bra her full breasts filled the lace cups of the camiknicker, swaying slightly as she moved. They hung lower than they would with a bra but her breasts were firm and she thought the effect soft and feminine. She had forgotten the suspender belt. Unclipping the camiknicker she pulled it up and fastened its clasp at her navel, twisting it round until the clasp was in the small of her back. The four suspenders hung down along her thighs. She unpacked the stockings and sat on the bed to draw them up her legs, careful not to ladder them. This was a strange sensation. She had only worn stockings three or four times in her life. They were associated for her with evening gowns and adolescent parties. Times when her mother had insisted that under the first long dress she had ever worn for her first formal dance she must wear stockings to make her feel 'right'. And they had. They'd made her feel special because all evening she had felt the strange elasticity around her thighs, the tugs and pulls and little nips to remind her this was not like other dances, parties, occasions. But no man had seen her like that. No man had got near her in that regalia. She was even afraid to sit down lest something became unattached — hook and eye, hairpin, mascara, high heel. So she was certainly not going to allow some man to do more than talk casually to her or dance stiffly with her, his hand firmly in the small of her back, their bodies well apart, her hand hardly touching the top of his shoulder. Nothing to damage the image so carefully prepared.

Very different now. She stood in front of the mirror, stockings smoothed into place, camiknicker refastened, the black high heels she had bought the other day on her feet. Quite a different approach from those virginal days. She had bought these stockings and put them on with the intention of wrapping her legs round Martin's back, so he could feel the rasp of nylon, so her cunt was stretched and open and he could push deep inside her. She had bought these stockings so he would kiss her from toe to cunt, lick the stockings, kiss the stockings, feel them, see them, want them. The image that men wanted. Looking at herself now, dressed like a sophisticated hooker, or so she thought, the tiny flickering impulses, almost like gentle needle pricks, began. She could feel the tightening of her nipples, she could see them erect under the soft lace of the camiknicker. The impulses receded or more accurately, they intensified until they joined into one continuous feeling of excited warmth.

Stephanie took the camiknicker off and stood looking at herself dressed only in the stockings and suspender belt and the shoes. She stood with her legs slightly apart, just enough to expose the pout of her nether lips covered in her downy pubic hair. The long fingers of the suspenders ran down her thighs, emphasising their shape, pulling the stockings up in arched peaks. The high heels made her ankles narrow, her calves tight. She turned her back to the mirror and looked over her shoulder. From the back the suspenders framed her arse like a picture, a black lace frame from the top of the stockings to the back of the suspender belt around her waist. A picture of ripe pink flesh split in two by the deep valley of her sex. She ran her hand over her buttocks down to the wisp of pubic hair showing at the back, as she might a sculpture, to feel the shape, the weight, the texture, the craft of it.

On an impulse she lay on the bed, drawing her knees up so she could hold her ankles with her hands. 'Like this,' she said out loud. Releasing her ankles she unbent her knees slightly and arched her back, raising her cunt off the bed like the mouth of an animal, a hungry animal. 'Like this?' Like the pictures she had seen in the magazines. The naked girls, their legs spread open, the stockings pulled tight, their cunts shiny and engorged.

She did not masturbate. She got up, took off the stockings and suspender belt and laid them carefully aside. She made herself a cup of tea, and rather to her surprise she found herself ringing George. Good old dependable George. She was certainly not burning her boats.

'Hallo George.'

'Darling how are you? Had a good day?'

'All right. You?'

'Not bad. Not much doing actually. Bit boring. Shall I come round? I've got nothing on.'

'No, not tonight. I've just washed my hair.'

'Tomorrow then?'

'Yes, all right.' What was she saying? 'No, no tomorrow's Tuesday.'

'It is. What's so special about Tuesday?'

'Make it Thursday.'

'What's so special about Tuesday?'

She hesitated. Suddenly she didn't want to lie about Martin. Why had she rung George?

'I've got things to do.'

'Very mysterious.'

'Thursday, then?'

'I haven't seen you . . .'

'Do you want to see me on Thursday?'

'Yes, all right. Don't get cross. I'd just like to see, you more often. We used to see a lot of each other.'

No, you used to see a lot of me while I got bored and looked the other way.

Not wanting to sit around doing nothing, knowing that would make the evening pass slowly, knowing she would once again start to think about Martin, she got dressed and went out to the wine bar two streets away from her flat. Several of her friends regularly put in an appearance there and she thought idle conversation would be good for her.

The wine bar, as wine bars, it seemed, had to be, was decorated throughout with a single motif — steam engines. Pistons, boilers, cylinders, gleaming brass plates, polished shovels and thousands of pictures of steam engines decorated every available surface. It was called, with the use of very little imagination, the Steam Inn. By the bar and a working scale model of a traction engine she spotted Penny who had already worked her way through two thirds of a bottle of the house red. She ordered another bottle and sat next to Penny who seemed a little the worse for wear. She was not an attractive girl and knew it. She had always found it difficult to attract men which she was desperate to do — did they sense her desperation and back away? Now, apparently, the man she had found two or three months ago had gone off without a word leaving her alone in the Steam Inn with her bottle of wine.

'I didn't think he'd do it. I didn't think he was that much of a bastard. I mean I knew something was up. He'd never take me out anywhere. Not even a drink. All he'd do is come round to my place or I'd go to his. He was ashamed of me, you see. Didn't want any of his friends to see him going out with a real dog. That was the reason. Good enough to fuck and that's it.'

'I'm sure that's not true.'

'Of course it's true. And I'll tell you something. I didn't mind in the least. He was so bloody good in bed

I couldn't have given a damn about going out. As long as he came round.'

'You can't base a relationship . . .'

'I could have. God, he just made me feel so good. He could do it for hours. On and on. I'd come so many times I'd lose count. I don't mean to be crude but it's true. He never seemed to get tired. He never seemed to go down, do you know what I mean?'

'Well I suppose . . .' Stephanie couldn't answer the question truthfully. Did she know? Perhaps the most truthful answer would have been 'Yes, almost . . .'

'I mean I didn't just lie there. God knows. I bet I was the best fuck he'd ever had. I gave him such a good time. It was electric. It takes two doesn't it? That's why I thought it would go on. He'd never get better anywhere else. None of his little county Sloanes would do what I did to him.'

'Perhaps he'll change his mind.'

Penny had drunk too much to listen so she sat back and injected the appropriate 'ah' or 'no' or 'really' and was glad of having nothing to do but listen. From Penny's long description of her sex life it occurred to her briefly that she was talking about Martin but then she mentioned his occupation and that line of thought dissolved. Suddenly the world was full of studs. Sex education, Dr Spock, an early acquaintance with Freud and the availability of sex manuals must be having an effect. Two out of twenty million.

'He loved me to put my finger in his arse. I don't mean to be crude. You know right up inside. Used to make him go wild.'

'While he's inside you?'

'If you've got long arms.' They both laughed.

'I haven't.'

'He said I was the first girl who'd ever done it to him.'

'No wonder he thought you were a good fuck.'

'He'll have to go a long way to find another woman who's prepared to do what I did.' She didn't elaborate any further. It might have been that there was nothing else to tell.

She'd have liked to cross-examine her on their sexual exploits. Pick-up tips. But Penny was too emotional for that and too drunk. Another night. File way the information that Penny was a source of sexual expertise.

She saw Penny home. Her flat was a mess. She made her a cup of the traditional strong black coffee but by the time she brought it into the front room Penny was asleep on the sofa. She let herself out and walked home a little nervously because of the time of night but not seriously doubting her safety. It was Tuesday tomorrow.

Why was it that the one person she should meet that night talked incessantly about sex? Was it Freud who said there was no accidents only causes for accidents?

8

Unfortunately Tuesday was a quiet day. She had wanted to be busy and occupied so she would not think of the evening. As she was quiet she thought of nothing else, so much so that by the end of the day she was almost bored with her fantasy, almost didn't want to be bothered with going through with it all as she had been through with it all so many times that day. She had walked up to the front door thirty times, and seen her hand reaching for the little illuminated door bell. Rang the door bell. Said the things she had planned to say to him. Smiled the way she had planned to smile. Looked around admiringly at the house, noticed herself noticing things. Things that were his, things that were his wife's. Carefully ignored things that were his wife's. Sat down in the proximity to him she had planned, asked for the drink she had decided to ask for (sherry with ice).

She had followed him upstairs, watched him take off his clothes. Waited until he was naked before she began to undress standing in front of him in the new black underwear. Seen his reaction. Kissed him. Sucked him. Fucked him. Taken him. Thirty times, forty times. That slow Tuesday.

She'd looked at the picture of his wife on the bedside table. Seen her robe hanging in the bathroom. Seen what perfume she preferred, what moisturiser, what cleanser, what colour toothbrush, what tampon; heard herself scream. And asked if he'd like help to change the sheets.

She had done it all that slow Tuesday sitting at her desk. To turn it into reality seemed almost too much effort. Almost.

She got into the back of the minicab. Sitting on the back seat she pulled her skirt down to make sure it creased as little as possible. She tried to evade the driver's attempts to make conversation.

'Off on the razzle, then.'

'Not really.'

'Look at 'em around here. More black than white. Surprised a girl like you lives around here. I mean I got nothing against them, I just wouldn't like to live next door to one.'

It felt strange wearing stockings. She could feel the backs of her thigh against the lining of her skirt. It felt as though wearing them had already made a statement about what she would, do with Martin, how she would feel. She felt open. The stockings made her feel open, her thighs naked and inviting.

'You see that programme on the telly last night? All those toerags down at the missile base. Not a lick of soap between the lot of 'em. They ought to cart 'em all away if you ask me. Don't suppose any of 'em have got an old man. Course most of 'em are Rita and Mike. You can see that. I don't hold with it. Do you hold with it miss.'

'I didn't see it.'

It was raining, a fine summer drizzle coating everything with a sheen of moisture. One of the stockings needed pulling up, the suspender was not tight enough now she was sitting down. She hadn't tried them sitting down, just walking about the flat. She couldn't do it now. The driver would hear, might even see in his mirror.

'. . . they've got their kids with 'em and all. I mean what are those kids goin' to grow up like, I ask you. I mean living in tents and all that squalor when you're a little nipper. That can't be good for you can it now? Can't be. There's one woman breast-feeding outside the tent you know, in front of the camera and everyone else for that matter. Right out in the open.'

Eventually he lapsed into silence and she could listen to the other noises. The wet tyres on the road, the gear changes, the wiper blades slapping each side of the windscreen. She had always loved that noise, ever since she was a child and drove in her father's old Morris Eight. The windscreen wipers were more rigid in those days, more upright and precise but they still made that regular slapping sound like a double metronome.

They were in the suburbs now. Large houses with gravel driveways, all two-car families. The large saloon and the little runabout. Roads tree-lined by virtue of the front garden trees leaning over their walls into the street. Then a section of terraced Victorian houses all studiously 'done-up'; restored to their imagined original glory. Her mind wandered well away from thoughts of Martin.

'Well it's been nice talking to you miss. One of the advantages of this job is getting to meet people. Putting the world to rights. Five pounds fifty.'

She paid him, giving six pounds. She couldn't tell whether he thought that was a poor tip or a good one and she really didn't care. As he drove off she hastily adjusted her stocking, looking up at the house to make sure he wasn't watching. Not entirely satisfied that she had been successful, she walked up the short path to the front door. She took little interest in the house. It was semi-detached and late Victorian and the front door had the original stained-glass panels and a large brass letter box.

As she stood in front of the door, hesitating before ringing the bell, she felt wicked, wanton and wild. The three w's. For a moment she felt so much that she had never felt before that it was as though she was not herself. It was as if someone else was standing there.

She rang the door bell. She counted the number of seconds to see how long it would take him to answer. Had he been waiting in the hall. Was he doing something else? Was he standing in the hall counting the seconds so it would appear as though he had been doing something else? Eleven seconds. She would never know. He opened the door.

'Hallo.'

'Come in.'

She walked past him into the hall. The door to the living room on the right was open and she walked in. He followed her, asked if she wanted a drink and went to get it. She didn't sit down or wander around the room looking at things. She didn't want to see their things. Not very brave. He came back with their drinks.

'Cheers.' He touched glasses.

'Why do people always do that?'

'It's to ward off evil spirits. The sound of the glass is supposed to scare them away.'

'Really?'

'We're obsessed by the need to protect ourselves from evil spirits. The earth must be lousy with them. Presumably as everything and everybody is in such a mess, the warding-off doesn't work and they have a field day.'

'Pessimist.'

'Joke.'

'What am I doing here?'

'Don't you know?'

'Are we going to eat?'

'Are you hungry?'

'No.'

'What do you want to do?'

'What is the respectable interval of small talk before I can get laid?'

'That's a very American expression.'

'You didn't answer.'

'The interval is already over.'

She kissed him. She put her tongue in his mouth until he pushed it back with his. She felt his erection against her. It was rock hard. How had he had time to get so excited? Was he excited before she'd arrived?

'You're very hard.'

'You excite me.'

'Thinking about me?'

'Yes. And the reality.'

'You're very hard.'

'For you.'

They kissed again. She ran her hand down to the front of his trousers and traced the shape of his penis pinching it to feel the hardness. She could feel her heartbeat racing.

'Why do you want me so much?'

'I don't know. Because you appear to want me too.'

'I do.'

'Do you want to go upstairs?'

'Yes, yes.'

'My God, I want you.'

76

'In the marital bed?'

'No.'

Martin led her upstairs into the guest room. She put her drink down on the bedside table and sat on the bed. He was standing in front of her, so she reached out and pulled down on his zip fly. The swollen penis made the zip difficult to undo or perhaps it was impatience. She wanted to see his penis, get it out and see it. She wormed her hand inside his trousers and clumsily, harshly pulled it clear of his pants so it stuck out of his trousers like the handle of a dagger by which he had been stabbed.

Almost as eagerly she plunged it into her mouth, licking it with long strokes of her tongue like a giant ice lolly, covering it with the wet of her saliva until it glistened. She noticed it was already weeping, its one eye producing the perfect teardrop.

As she licked she used her hands to free his balls. She wanted to lick those too, but that was enough for him and he pulled away, undoing the top button of his trousers and letting them fall. Then he sat on the bed next to her and pulled his shoes and socks off — perfectly trained in the art of undressing — before he stood to take his pants and trousers off. His penis jutted just below the level of his shirt.

This time she fell to her knees to take it in her mouth again. His balls were free and she moved her mouth down the stem of his penis until she could feel the hair around the base and lick at his sac. Gently she manoeuvred them one by one into her mouth, until she could feel the delicate oval ball securely in her mouth, a giant lozenge to be sucked, not chewed.

He was moaning. She was using her hand to wank him slowly as her mouth worked at his balls. She could feel another sticky wet tear roll from the eye of his penis. She could feel it pulse against her cheek, feel its heat, its energy and its desire as she sucked gently on his balls one after another and pulled on the long stem of flesh.

'You're making me come.'
'Come.'
'No.'
'I want you too.'
'Not yet.'

He took her head and pulled it away from him. He looked down into her eyes.

Stephanie stood up and he took off his shirt and lay on the bed his legs apart, one leg drawn up slightly, his penis erect, the bag of his balls hanging down between his legs. She unbuttoned her blouse and hung it carefully on a chair. She unzipped the skirt, let it fall to the floor and stepped out of it. Picking it up she made sure her bottom faced him and he could see the straight seams of her black stockings.

'Unbutton me,' she said coming over to the bed.
He looked puzzled. 'Where?'
'Between my legs. There's clasps.'

Tentatively at first he ran his hand over the front of the camiknicker and down between her legs. He found what he was looking for.

'So there is.'

He fumbled to undo the clasps. He told her he wanted to pull her on to the bed and plunge into her. He told her he had never seen a more sexy sight. The long black stockinged legs, the black high heels. And now fumbling between her legs to free her cunt, as if he was opening a long awaited present – the excitement making the fingers awkward with the wrapping. Her heat, he told her, he could feel her heat.

When the last clasp was undone she pulled the

camiknicker over her head without moving away from him. Her breasts fell free. She stood in the stockings and suspenders, her legs slightly apart.

'Men are supposed to like stockings. Do you?'

'Yes.'

'Do you?'

'Yes.'

'I'm hot. I'm wet. I have dreams of you.'

'I know.'

'I have never felt like this. I don't know what it is.'

'I know. Look at me. Don't you think I feel the same?'

'Lie there. Don't touch me. Will you?'

'Will I what?'

'Will you do as I say?'

'Yes.'

'I want you to do as I say. That's what I dreamt.'

She had dreamt. But the reality was more, bigger, greater, more intoxicating. The reality was the sight of him, his body, his penis. The reality was the words, the deeds. The blood, the lust, the feeling of her heart racing, beating against her ribs.

'What do you want me to do?'

'Don't move. Don't touch me.'

'I want to.'

'Do as I say.'

'All right.'

As if to test his obedience she ran her hand down the length of his penis. As an afterthought she gathered the new tear that had appeared at its tip on to her finger and put her finger in her mouth. She sucked on it elaborately but couldn't taste anything. He watched without moving. She knelt on the bed, careful not to snare her high heels in the bedclothes. She wanted to keep them on.

She reached out and took his penis in her fist. Using it like a handle she pivoted her weight over him until she knelt with her knees either side of his thighs, centring herself on his penis. She was intensely aware of her cunt in a way she had never been before. It seemed to be alive like a separate being controlling her, telling her what to do, how it wanted to be, where it wanted to be. She seemed to be able to feel it, the lips, her clitoris, the length of her vagina: feel its heat and its wetness, its feelings expressed by heat and wet: its own language. She could feel it now opening ready for him, the nether lips swollen, fanning open like the shell of a clam ready to snap shut on him.

She could feel her breasts too. They felt heavy, heavier than she could remember. She could feel her nipples puckered and hard; hard like iron and cold like iron, every wrinkle around the central bud like the texture of a sculpture in stone, rough and ungiving. They felt like they were caught forever erect, would never be flaccid again.

She looked down at him. She had never felt this way. She had already behaved in a way she had never behaved before. Any inhibition she had ever had about sex was gone now as she knelt before him. She could do anything, was capable of anything. There were no limits. A wave of exhilaration overcame the sexual excitement. No limits. No regrets. No wondering what could or could not be done, should or should not be said.

She had never touched herself in front of a man. She put her finger down between her legs now, parted the lips of her cunt and stroked her clitoris. She had never licked the juices of her body in front of a man. She took her fingers from her clitoris and licked it. This time the taste was strong, a salted muskiness. She had never sucked her nipples in front of a man. She took her breast in her hand now and pulled it to her mouth bending her head until she could take the nipple and suck the iron flesh. The exhilaration returned. There were no limits.

For a moment she had almost forgotten him. As if Martin had had the same thought he reached up to touch the nipple she had just sucked, the nipple still glistening with her saliva.

'No.' She swayed back out of his reach.
'Why not?'
'Do as I say.'
'I want to touch you.'
'Later, it will be your turn.'
'Turn?'
'This is my turn. Don't you like it?'

She caught his penis in her fist and squeezed. At the same time she moved the pouting lips of her cunt until the tip of his penis nestled in her pubic hair. Her cunt's response was immediate, an eloquent speech of approval delivered in words of heat and moist juices. Rolling her buttocks to and fro she rubbed the penis hard against her clitoris. He moaned a little uncomfortably, she thought, the pubic hair caught against his sensitive skin, a moan that contained a hint of when are you going to stop?

'Would you like me to hurt you? Does pain turn you on?'

She had no idea if giving pain would turn her on.
'I don't know.'
'Should I try?' Did she really want to try? She ground against his penis again.
'It's your turn.' He smiled.

She didn't want to see him smile. As a way of stopping him, stopping him instantly she dropped her weight on to him and his penis sunk to the hilt in the ribbed warmth of her cunt. The smile disappeared. Or perhaps it hadn't, but for her it had because the action of his penis had forced her to close her eyes to wallow in the sensation, to listen to her cunt and all the other senses. She could feel him totally. She seemed to be able to feel every curve, every ridge, every throbbing vein of his penis inside her — she knew in fact, in some other mind of some other person that dealt with facts, that this was not possible. But that is what she felt now. She felt as though he had joined her, become part of her. Her penis. She tried to concentrate on where she ended and he began but there was no join, just feeling.

Very slowly she raised her cunt and let him slide out of her a little. Then back down again until he was at the neck of her womb. Then out, a little further out this time. And back, out and back. A long complex journey full of adventures, full of swirling storms and rocky rapids to be negotiated and overcome. Out and back. Out until he was almost at her nether lips, out until her cunt begged for him back again, to swallow him again in its damp silky walls.

'Don't move, don't do anything. Don't touch me. Don't do anything. I want to do it all. I want to move it. I want to fuck you. Just let me do it to you.' She wanted to say other things, things about his penis, things about his sperm, things about his sperm coming into her, filling her, dripping into her but she could not concentrate on saying them, only on thinking them. Her eyes were closed and inside her head she could do nothing but think of him coming, the spurts of white hot sperm pouring into her, hitting the back walls of her cunt's lightless caverns like jets of cream. She could see his penis tensing to come, see the veins swell finally, see the sperm shoot out against the walls of her vagina. A graphic picture in living colour. See it all in her mind.

She was moving faster now. Out and back the whole length of his penis, the whole length of her cunt. Plunging herself down on him. She opened her eyes to look at him. His eyes were closed, his face set in an expression that looked more like pain than pleasure. She looked at herself. Looked down at her breasts bouncing up and down in time to her hips. Looked at the suspenders straining at the top of the stockings and her high heels clinging precariously to her toes, the heels off and loose.

Once more. In once more. Out and back. Back once more. Once more and she would come.

'Come, come. Come now. Come now.'

Was she imagining it? Could she feel his penis tense, could she feel the tip swell? Out and back. Suddenly he moved. He was pushing into her against the rhythm she had set up. Faster than her rhythm. Out and back. But not so far out as she had taken it, and back more urgently. He was coming, wanting to make sure he came inside her, right up inside her, in the right place, the good dark place. He was finding his place.

It was knowing that that made her come. She was lost then, lost as she had never been. Her cunt was convulsing, out of control, squeezing on him, opening for him, contracting to him, pulsing around him, each movement sending her into ecstasy. It was the closest pleasure had ever come to pain. Wave on wave diminishing as her cunt lost it impetus and stopped milking his penis for its thick white cream.

In the middle of her orgasm she had supposed she felt him come but to be honest she could not remember. The impact of her own feelings had been too much.

She knelt over him, his penis still inside her. Oddly she could not feel it now. Perhaps it had already softened. He was looking at her.

She felt his penis slide out of her though, like an overfed worm caught out on the lawn by a hungry bird and trying to wriggle to safety. She looked down at it, all small and unattractive now and looking as though it had been caught in a rain storm, soaked to the skin and all the pubic hair pressed down and wet too.

An awkward moment. The embarrassment of unbridled lust slacked. A vacuum of feeling. Nature abhors a vacuum.

'Drink?'

'Please.'

He got off the bed and naked went downstairs. He did not look back at her or try to say anything else. She smiled wanly at him but she didn't think he saw her smile and was quite glad he hadn't.

She took off her shoes and lay on the bed raising her legs in the air one at a time to straighten the stockings. Her legs felt sweaty and damp. Nature's way of telling you to slow down. She smiled at the thought of the old joke. Death is nature's way of telling you to slow down. Orgasm is nature's way of telling you to slow down. Her heartbeat was still not back to normal. She didn't want to think about what had happened. That was strange. She just wanted it to go on. Then she would think about it. On and on.

She supposed there was an end, an outer limit, only because everything had an end. Even infinity.

9

When Martin came back he had put on a robe, presumably taken from the marital bedroom. Should she insist they fuck on the marital bed? He was smiling.

'Smug again?'
'That's not why I was smiling.'
'Why then?'
'It's my turn.'

They drank and lay back on the bed in silence for a moment. They lay side by side but didn't hold hands or embrace.

'What does your turn involve?'
'Are you always like this?'
'Like what?'
'Uninhibited.'
'Is that what I am?'
'Yes.'
'Always meaning what?'
'With other men.'
'You wouldn't believe me if I told you.'
'I would.'
'I don't think I want to tell you.'
'Is it a secret?'

That was not her secret. Stephanie sat up and took another sip of her drink.

'I seem to have developed a sudden interest in sex. I mean a fascination. I want to explore it. Get to know it. Collect it like collecting stamps, different nationalities . . .'

'Different men?'

'No, not different men.'

'What, then?'

'I don't know. It's since meeting you, I think. Since the first time. No, that's not quite true, it was beginning before. I was beginning to read things.'

'Things?'

'Books, books on sex. Kinky sex. Do you know some men want women to pee in their mouths?'

'Is that what you want to do?'

'I'm serious.'

'Serious question.'

'No, but it interests me. It interests me that there seem to be so many different sexual experiences. Rubber suits, leather, being whipped, men wearing women's clothes . . .'

'It's fantasy. Sex in the mind. Sex is a fantasy.'

'What's fantastic about dressing up in rubber?'

'Not the reality. It's a symbol. It represents something.'

'What?'

'I don't know. Whatever turned them on once. Whatever has become the release, the trigger, the thing that turns sex into another . . . dimension. Hasn't it ever occurred to you? Animals fuck to reproduce. Man doesn't. Not any more. Not for a long time. Man does it for pleasure. Sometimes, if not all the time, purely for pleasure. So it's lost its *raison d'etre*. There is literally no reason to have sex any more. Children can be produced without it. So we have to find a new reason. And it's not easy. Pleasure is a reason. But what if we all get bored with pleasure? Too much of a good thing. Boredom. We need another dimension, something unobtainable, something to aim for, something it's almost impossible to get.'

'A fantasy?'

'Yes. Because fantasy never becomes reality.'

'So the world is full of people turning their back on straight sex and buying rubber knickers?'

'No. The world is full of people turning their back on sex, full stop.'

'I thought infidelity was rife.'

'Same thing. One night stands have very little to do with sex, don't they?'

'I thought kinky sex was supposed to come from some childhood trauma.'

'Early Freud.'

'Yes.'

'I'm sure he's right. But the people you're talking about don't suffer from one thing.'

'What?'

'Boredom.'

She laughed. She wasn't sure how serious he was being or whether his theory was something he just made up to pass the time while they 'changed ends', but she was glad it was possible to have some sort of conversation with him.

'Do you have a fantasy?' he asked.

'Women aren't supposed to have fantasies. They're supposed to be straightforward. Simple uncomplicated sex. No frills. No hang-ups like men.'

'And?'

'I must have had a trauma in childhood.'

'So what's your fantasy?'

For a moment she wondered if it were a good idea to tell him the truth.

'As close as it is possible we've just performed my current fantasy.'

He laughed. 'Then it's only fair that we now perform mine.'

He kissed her on the mouth, not a sexy kiss at all. A tender kiss, a tongue barely penetrating the mouth kiss. Very gently he stroked her breast, avoiding the nipple. And then the other breast, but this time stroking the nipple until it sprang up and he could grasp it between two fingers and squeeze just that little bit to hard.

'What happens if the idea revolts me?'

'It won't.'

'How do you know?'

'I know.'

And she knew absolutely that it wouldn't. She knew because she could not believe anything he did to her she would not want.

'Are you a closet transvestite?'

'Would you mind?'

She was just about to say 'no' flippantly when she heard the question again in her mind. Would she mind if he lay on her wearing a bra stuffed with old socks and a suspender belt and stockings over his hairy legs and little white cotton knickers from which he had extracted his penis to push between her legs in her stockings. Nylon on nylon.

'No,' she lied.

He left the room. From next door she could hear drawers opening and closing, cupboards swing open. She lay on the bed and opened her legs slightly. Don't think about it now, think about it later, she told herself. Both her nipples had remained erect from his last touch and now she felt her cunt swim back to the surface of life, the nether lips seeming to flex slightly, beginning to ready themselves, tumescence returning. For what we are about to receive . . .

He stood at the door, one hand behind his back.

'Close your eyes.'

She obeyed, hearing him cross the room and sit on the bed, dropping whatever he held on the floor. She heard a rustle of cloth.

'All right.' She opened them again. He had put a red scarf, one of his wife's, over the bedside lamp.

'Not that it matters,' he said, explaining the remark by producing a little black sleeping mask. 'Lift your head.' She obeyed again and he slipped the mask over her head and down over her eyes. She was blindfolded. A sensation of pleasure ran through her so instantly that it made her catch her breath. She could hear the words echoing in her mind. *'Lift your head.'* Not a request. An order, surrounded by duty and obligation. Her heart was beating faster in her dark black world. She could almost see it beating. She opened her eyes. A very faint glimmer of red light came from the edges of the black silk but she could see nothing else. Only hear.

She heard him take off his robe, or assumed that was what she heard, then felt his weight on the bed. He pulled her forward and piled pillows behind her head. Now he was kneeling in front of her. She could feel his knees either side of her waist and then the touch of his penis, his penis erect again, between her breasts. Then he raised himself higher and she felt his penis brush the lips of her mouth.

'Take it.'

'No.' She was playing the game.

'Take it.' Harder. Stronger. She could not refuse.

'I can't.'

'Do as I say.'

He pulled her head forward on to his penis. She sucked it into her mouth. He was fully erect and hot. Blood heat. He pushed into her so she could do nothing but contain him. That was what he wanted. He pulled back and in again holding her head with his hand at the back of her neck. Was he going to come? He felt hot enough to come.

As she sucked his penis she felt her cunt. Felt her heart and her cunt. Her heart was fluttering as though the excitement was too much for it. Her mind explained gently to her that all that was happening was that she was giving a man a blow job while she happened to be wearing a blindfold, but it had no impact, no calming effect. Her heart knew differently and so did her cunt. She eased her legs further open to give it more room to play, more room to flex and swell. She could feel its heat, radiating out between her thighs, and she was sure she was sitting in a stain of wet on the sheet. She could feel her cunt, her nether lips, her clitoris throb. As she sucked the gourd of his flesh it seemed to her so like her clitoris, swollen, hot and needing attention, needing release.

He pulled back withdrawing his penis from her mouth. She gave an involuntary gasp and turned her head from side to side as if trying to locate it again.

'No. That is only the beginning.'

'I wanted you to come.'

'My turn.'

'You don't want that?'

'Don't talk.'

Stephanie felt the weight lift from the bed as he got up. For a moment she wanted to end the game, tear the blindfold off, kiss him on the mouth and return to normal, take him in her again normally, properly. That desire didn't last for long. She blinked her eyes feeling them catch against the material of the blindfold and heard the rustle of material. The excitement returned. The sense of expectation.

'Put your hands together,' he ordered.

'Why?'

'Don't ask questions.' His voice was cold, stern.

She put her hands together on her navel. Her fingertips rested against the top of her pubic hair. She could feel it was still slightly damp. There was a noise of movement and then she felt a silky cloth on her wrists, pulling them together and binding them. He was tying her hands. She could feel her heart start to thump again, her breathing become shallow, in short little pants. He was tying her up.

He pulled her hands up over her head and tied them to the wooden headboard of the bed. The bonds were not tight but when she wriggled her wrists slightly she knew they were real enough. She could not get free. She could not get free. Supposing he was a rapist . . . Inwardly she laughed at the thought. She'd just given him her body freely, she had no intention of changing her mind now. He could be a murderer. He might slit her throat. Stab her. Maim her . . .

She felt him reach for her ankle. A soft material snaked round it and then she felt it pulled to one side and tied down to the leg of the bed. When he tied the other ankle she would be open. Open. For a moment there was silence. What was he doing. Looking down at her from the foot of the bed? Watching her? Silence. She started slightly when she felt the brush of his fingertip against her left nipple. It made her realise how erect it was, made her aware that her body had no misgivings as to his intentions.

She lay on the bed, her legs spread-eagled, her cunt open. Open to his gaze, open to his fingers, open to his penis, his mouth. Open. My God, she was excited. She realised she was beginning to breathe slowly, deeply. Breathing out through her nose. His fingers were touching her nipple again. Then they stopped. She turned her head trying to sense where he was. She could not. A hot wet tongue flickered at her nipple. Both nipples one after another.

Then he was gone. She heard him walk across the room and close the door. Perhaps he hadn't gone. Perhaps he was standing inside the door watching to see what she would do, what she could do. She listened intently. As far as she could tell he was gone. She listened again. He was gone.

For a second she felt vaguely ridiculous. Is this what he did with his wife on Sunday afternoon after roast beef and Yorkshire pudding? Where was he? What was he doing now? She tried to pull her legs up but apart from a couple of inches of leeway they were firmly tied. Her hands too. Another badge for knots no doubt. She had a desire to touch herself, to touch her cunt and her breasts. And she could not. She could not touch and she could not see.

But Stephanie could feel. She could feel her breasts stretched out over her chest, her nipples taut and hard. She could feel the lips of her cunt, open and swollen. She could feel her damp pubic hair. She could feel her mouth and taste him where he had been. And by moving her legs to the maximum the bonds allowed and by squeezing her thighs together she could compress her nether lips, compress them enough to rub her clitoris slightly, rhythmically. Compress and release. Such a tiny movement but held as she was, blind as she was, it was a movement that thrilled her out of all proportion to its size.

She stopped when the door opened and he came back to stand by the bed. He did not speak. His weight pulled the bed down as he climbed up to kneel between her open legs. He leant forward, his hands either side of her head and poked up into her with his penis. It didn't find her opening at first, banging into her clitoris and then on to one side of her labia. Third time lucky. Inside her. Her cunt wet and ready. All the way in. And out. In and out.

Was it Martin? Had he gone downstairs to get someone off the street? The next-door neighbour. Listen, I've got this girl tied up on my bed, would you fancy a quick fuck? Sexy little piece. She felt her cunt responding to Martin, if it was him, squeezing him, moulding itself to him, becoming part of him. This orgasm was different. She could feel herself coming right from his first penetration. It was just a question of climbing the ladder, each of his strokes a rung. Like seconds ticking off. Twenty more to go. Each second stronger, harder, warmer. A deep heat spreading out from her cunt to every part of her. Warmer and warmer each second. Was this a stranger? Was she being fucked by a total stranger. A cock she'd never seen. Some misshapen, hideous, obscene, wiry-haired cock fucking her now. Inside her soft precious cunt. Five more seconds. She knew he was coming too, coming with her. She was melting inside, melting over him. So hot. She knew he could not hold out against her heat. And his fantasy.

They came together. She heard herself scream as she gushed over him and he into her. She wanted to hug him to her and she could not. She wanted to see him and she could not. She wanted to close her legs and she could not.

'Have you done that before?'

'Once.'

She could not believe that was the truth. 'With your wife?'

'God, no.'

'Who, then?'

'A girl.'

'Who?'

'She was called Anne.'

'Did she like it?'

'Why do you want to know?'

'Did she like it?'

'I think so. We only did it the once.'

'It's a very strange sensation.'

'Don't analyse it.'

'Why?'

'I don't think you should. Isn't the feeling enough?'

'Yes.'

'Well?'

'What I was saying before. I have to think something about all this, don't I? I have never felt this way before. I've never had . . . Do all your women tell you this?'

'No.'

'You wouldn't tell me.'

'I have been complimented on my performance. That's not what you mean, is it?'

'No. I don't know. Maybe it is.'

They had both got dressed and gone downstairs. He made them bacon sandwiches and tea. She felt awful immediately she had dressed. She felt shaky and though she hated to admit it, nauseous. She wanted to go home. At first it was a passing fancy but in a short time it had become a raging desire. She wanted to go home and go to bed. She wanted to forget what had happened or at least to lose it in the oblivion of sleep.

'You don't look too good.'
'It'll end in tears . . .'
'What?'
'Too much excitement.'
'Do you want to go?'
'When does your wife get back?'
'Tomorrow. You could stay.'
'No.' She said it rather too quickly.
'Now you've had your wicked way with me, you mean.' He smiled.
'No. I don't feel well. Really.'
'I'd run you . . .'
'I'd rather get a taxi.'

She did. Her sense of confusion was increasing. The best thing was not to think about it. Go home and go to bed. Sleep. Perfect dreamless sleep. Go home and go to bed. But what was she doing? Why didn't she want to stay with him, talk to him, be with him. She had wanted him so much physically and now she could barely stand to talk to him. No, that wasn't true. It was just that she felt so ill and it was getting worse every minute. The potion's wearing off, Miss Hyde. She told herself she would have loved to stay the night, to be with him. Hug him. Cuddle him. Make love again in the morning. But she could not tell if that was true or not. She just felt ill.

'Do you want to meet again?'
'Look, I really feel terrible.'
'I know.'
'I'd have liked to stay . . .'
'Is this the brush off . . .?'
'No.'
'We could have a weekend. Go away somewhere.'

10

It was a dream. But it was not the dream she would have expected. She was not strapped down on the sacrificial altar, white pleated dress ripped off her breast as men, bronzed athletic muscle-bound men, their heads covered with masks made from the heads of horned animals, their bodies oiled and naked, masturbated over her while their high priest/chief/witch doctor crammed his massive phallus into her open and prone cunt.

Stephanie was naked in her dream She was in a field. In the middle distance she could see a small neat farmhouse and she thought she could smell, faintly on the slightest breeze, bread baking in an oven. She had had no feeling of embarrassment at her nudity and no feeling that she needed to be clothed if someone should come along. What she was doing in the field she had no idea. Nor did she know where her clothes were. It seemed so natural to be naked that it was difficult to imagine wearing clothes at all. A man did walk by at one point. He was fully dressed and saw her clearly but made no attempt to stare or do more than say a polite hello. He obviously thought her nakedness was as natural as she did.

In the house — in the way of dreams she couldn't remember walking to the house — she sat at the table. There were other people there to eat but she could only sense them, not see them or know who they were. There was nothing ominous or sinister in their presence. They were just there. The meal was delicious.

Back in the field, with the feeling of contentment associated with food, she felt a surge of energy and started to climb an old oak tree. She had always climbed trees as a girl. She enjoyed working out the best route up through the branches, enjoyed the feeling of the rough knotted bark and the views when she got as high as she could safely go. The old oak was an easy climb but she did not remember getting anywhere near its top. She woke in her bedroom.

The relaxation and contentment that the dream had given her lasted all day. It was like a marvellous aftertaste of food to be called up whenever desired. It informed her, made her smile. The feeling of nausea was gone, gone so completely she could hardly remember what it had felt like. A product of the mind brought on stage by some protective mechanism — some overload circuit — or was that just a psychological cliché?

She did not see Martin that day. She did not think of him either. George rang and asked if she'd have dinner with her that night instead of Thursday. She agreed readily. Funnily enough that was exactly what she wanted. Good old George. Good old dependable George. She had had enough excitement for one week. George would quickly restore her boredom threshold.

'What time?'

'Eight.'

'You all right?'

'Why?'

'Just wondered.'
'Why?'
'No reason.'
'I feel terrific. Is that what it is? Perhaps you're not used to hearing me in this mood.'
'What have you been up to then?'
'Nothing. Just a general sense of wellbeing.'
'Eight then.'
'Bye.'

The men in the office would put a 'general sense of wellbeing' down to being well and satisfyingly fucked, the masculine answer to any woman's problem. The fact that in her case this seemed to be patently true annoyed her temporarily. The tiniest of clouds passed over the expanse of blue sky. Is that what George would think? Not that she really cared what he thought. He had certainly never been responsible for even the slightest suggestion of wellbeing. Irritation, yes.

But George served his turn. And she had a specific turn for him tonight. What was it they called it in O level chemistry — a control. In one culture dish you applied the new agent and in the other you left everything untouched. So you could compare the changes. George was the control. So she could observe the changes. She smiled to herself. Science was a wonderful thing.

On the tube there was something about the familiarity of her routine, the same place on the platform, the familiar faces in the carriage mixed with the unfamiliar, the same sequence of stations, that unsettled her. It was not as reassuring as she might have expected. It reminded her that what had happened last night was quite out of the ordinary, non-routine, anything but familiar.

Visions of herself floated into her mind, however

much she attempted to dismiss them. Of course, as she had been blindfolded, the visions were necessarily imaginary and her mind no doubt dramatically embroidered the truth. She saw herself lying tied to the bed, her legs pulled apart, muscles straining, arms, elbows, bent above her head, her cunt wet and open. She could see the bonds cutting down into her ankles, her wrists. She saw them as white silk. She had no idea what they actually were — Martin had been careful to untie her before removing the blindfold. He had put the bonds away by the time she could see again. If she had been tied untidily with a collection of old school ties and scarves that was not how she saw it in her mind's eye. In her mind's eye the bonds were silky, uniform, precise. Nothing squalid and improvised. In her mind's eye there was a ritual quality to her bondage and the accoutrements were therefore objects of the ritual, sacred and pristine, pressed to the lips, like priestly robes, before application.

She had drifted so far away the noise of the tube doors jolting open suddenly reminded her she had no idea where she was. Twisting round to find the station sign she realised to her relief she had not gone past her stop. Two more. For a second the woman sitting opposite caught her eye. A passing flicker, of what? Recognition? Sympathy? Sisterhood? The eyes moved away.

It was Stephanie's secret. It was fascinating to look fleetingly at the woman opposite, to think of her sexuality. What was her secret? What lay hidden behind the placid exterior she was presenting to the world? She was roughly the same age as Stephanie. Objectively she was not as obviously attractive. She was heavier, not fat, but padded with an extra layer of flesh. Her ankles were rounder, her hips fuller, her cheeks chubbier. But her eyes sparkled and her body suggested an easy confidence in her own reactions.

Stephanie had always been fascinated by the thought of what people did in private. Since she had read the books she realised that there were almost no limits to the sexual imagination. What was her secret, this chipper mousy-haired woman? Did her husband/boyfriend/lover dress from head to toe in thin black latex in order to get an erection? Did she whip him with birch twigs, walk over him in six-inch stiletto heels? Did her man bring home his friend and did they fuck her alternately – or simultaneously – one in her mouth, the other in her cunt?

Another thought occurred to her. It would be difficult to discuss her experience with any of her friends. How are you? Oh, I'm fine, I've met this marvellous man who ties me to the bed and gives me the best orgasms I've had in my life. It was Stephanie's secret. And it would have to stay that way. If the woman opposite whipped her man to orgasm that was probably her secret too.

Their eyes met again, a longer look. Stephanie smiled the faintest of smiles which the woman returned then looked away.

Maybe it was like a dam holding back the flood. If she told Joyce or Penny or any of her friends would they in turn suddenly divulge the intimate secrets of an outlandish sex life? If she thought about it there was really nothing to discuss with her friends. She didn't want to tell them for support, for approval or as a sort of strange boost. She had discussed her boredom with George only because she knew that Joyce's response would be exactly what she wanted to hear – amused sympathy and understanding for the thankless lot of women when faced with the unsophisticated and unaware man. But this was not a matter for discussion precisely because she had no idea what Joyce's reaction would be and ultimately she had no wish to find out.

She would tell no one. At least not at this stage. At least not without provocation. Her secret. A fine and private place.

Damn. This time as the tube doors opened she realised she had missed her stop. Leaping up she pushed out through the doors not having time for a final look at the woman she had touched briefly with her eyes. Not time for the final look that would have said goodbye. Why were goodbyes so important? Another unanswered question.

At home she went through her home-coming routine. So much of life was routine. Carefully ordered sequences of totally meaningless events. Thinking of Joyce on the train had reminded her that she hadn't seen her for weeks, and certainly not since Martin. That was the disadvantage – or advantage – of living alone; there was no instant conference to digest the latest developments, no analysis, dissections, postmortems over gin, coffee, shopping lists. No little admissions, little truths wrought before consideration developed the inhibitions to counsel silence. A conspiracy of silence. A brooding silence. Alternatively, she thought, smiling to herself at the idea, a secret dark exciting silence, full of half formed thoughts, anticipation and expectation.

Still she would give Joyce a ring. It would be fun to see her again. And talk.

She had made tea in a small teapot, just enough for one. Putting the teapot on a little tray she had set, one cup, one saucer, one jug of milk, one tea strainer, she carried it though into the living room and put it on the occasional table next to her chair — the chair she always sat in.

The tea was too weak. She took a large sip then topped up the cup from the teapot. Better. So precise, her requirements. It was probably true that if she was still living with one of the girls the current situation would be different. But what was the current situation? It was nothing more than a sexual infatuation for one particular man. The other things were incidentals, the product of an overactive imagination as her mother would have said. There was nothing wrong with sexual infatuation. It was true that she had never felt it quite so strongly before but then she had never met a man who had been such a good lover before. 'Good lover' was a misnomer. He had discovered, subliminally, subvocally, telepathetically, inter-murally, subconsciously that at this particular time she was not looking for another sexual liaison ending, at its imaginative best, in combinations of six and nine. He had known she wanted more, and he had given her more almost before she knew she wanted it. And that was the cause of her infatuation.

Quite simple. Nothing to worry about there. Not a psychotic obsession as the result of a prolonged periods of loneliness. Not a product of loneliness. That was other people's concern, not her own. Other people's worry. 'Aren't you lonely?' 'You must get so lonely.' People seemed to fear loneliness like some terminal disease, talking about it as if it were a disease to be avoided at all costs. She did not get lonely living on her own. She had herself. And now she had a hobby. Sex.

George had picked her up at eight and taken her to dinner. She was very hungry. She listened to George's endless monologue of missed financial opportunities, nodding automatically in the appropriate places and occasionally drifting off into thoughts of Martin.

With as much grace as he possessed he explained as they drank coffee that he had to deliver some documents to a client before he took her home. (Why didn't he say before he fucked her?) It wasn't out of their way.

They drove in silence for once. It wasn't far from the restaurant, a large Georgian house, beautifully restored, a very expensive house in a very expensive area. George got out of the car.

'Won't be a minute.'

'O.K.'

He walked to the front door and she watched as it opened for him and closed after him. A few seconds later it opened again and George came plodding back to the car.

'We're invited in for brandy.'

'I'm not dressed . . .'

'You look fine.'

'Another time . . .'

'Come in . . .'

He opened the car door. She would not have been badgered had she not seen the man waiting at the door watching the proceedings. She had no wish to appear churlish.

'Hello.'

'This is Mr Devlin.'

To her surprise he took her hand and kissed it. He looked into her eyes as his lips touched the back of her hand. He was a man of sixty, curly wiry black hair laced with grey, slim with a natural grace of movement. His clothes were expensive as were his surroundings. He was also the ugliest man Stephanie had ever seen.

His nose was enormous, his mouth curled and asymmetrical, his ears almost half the length of his head with long bulbous lobes. He had hair growing from his ears, from his nose, from his cheek, above the line where he shaved, and from under his collar, up to the point where his razor cut it away. Only his eyes, a deep brown, had any appearance of normality.

He had seen her response many times before, she knew. He made no attempt to look away as she reacted to his face. He seemed to welcome the fact that his face made it almost irresistible to stare and stare and stare. He must know by now the absolute fascination of true ugliness.

He poured their drinks into crystal glass and offered them a tour of the house. It was a beautiful house and she oohed and aahed in all the right places. The money had clearly been no object. But it was money used with considerable taste. In the bedroom, on the wall opposite the bed, there was a large oil. She did not know the artist. It was the most erotic painting she had ever seen.

George and Devlin had gone on to the next room. She stood staring into the full-sized oil. At first she had thought it was an abstract with wild bright colours; but then she realised that the lines and shades of deepest red towards the centre were in fact the most exquisite representation of a vulva. Following out from this centre it was then possible to make out the long curved thighs of a woman's opened legs. She was lying on her back, her legs drawn up, her knees bent. A man, or a least the impression of a man, for all that could be seen was a round hollow face and the long curve of the spine, the knuckles of the vertebrae pushing out, knelt between the legs facing the open cunt; not touching it, not looking, his eyes glazed and sightless.

As she stared another figure emerged from the abstraction. Standing over the woman was another woman, her hair long and jet black. She was naked with long pendulous breasts, and though there were no features, no detail, she gave the impression of being older. One of her long breasts touched the shoulder of the lying woman and her eyes looked down to be met by the other woman's eyes as she twisted her head round and looked up − a long immobile stare. There was no impression that the women were touching, other than the casual touch of the older woman's breast. Three figures locked in some sexual rite, held together by the depth of crimson.

The eye was drawn back to that crimson vulva. It seemed to be on fire. It seemed to be a bottomless pit of colour, the perfect expression of the sexual act. For some reason it was clear that this tableau was after the act. The woman lying down had been fucked, sucked, had. Now she lay open, her spent passion coloured her cunt. She needed to say nothing. All that needed to be said lay there before the other two − in shades of red.

'Beautiful isn't it?'

She had not heard him come back into the room and had no idea how long he'd been watching her.

'Wonderful.'

'George is having a pee.'

He put his hand lightly on her breast.

'Does it affect you?'

It did, it had. She actually felt breathless. She put her hand on his but not as a rebuke.

'Yes. It's incredibly sexy. I've never seen anything like it.'

'There are so many stories, aren't there. What are they doing? Who are they all? What is their relationship? It's a great game to play lying in bed at night. Better than counting sheep.'

'I'm sure it is.'

He withdrew his hand. 'Come back.'

'Sorry?'

'Come back. Drop George off and come back here.'

'I couldn't.'

'Why?'

'I couldn't.'

'Shouldn't you be outraged at the suggestion?'

'Yes.'

'But you're not?'

'You're right. I should be.'

George came back into the room. If he was aware of an atmosphere he did not show it. He seemed hardly to have noticed the painting. He thanked Devlin for the tour and the use of the bathroom and said they must be going. At the front door Devlin remembered he had promised to lend her a book. She did not protest at the fabrication. Nothing had been said about a book. He reappeared with a little book of paintings by the man who had painted the oil in the bedroom. She thanked him and said she'd return it. He said there was no need.

'I didn't ask you what it was called,' she said outside on the porch at the top of the steps.

'Do you want to guess?'

'Ah . . . After.'

'I know what you mean. Actually it's called "Complex".'

'Much more enigmatic.'

'Much more speculative.'

George asked her, in the car, what they had been talking about.

'The painting in the bedroom.'

He lost interest immediately.

The image of the centre of the painting, that crimson vulva, like an exotic tropical orchid variegated from the lightest pink to the deepest crimson, a crimson almost black where the labia parted slightly to reveal the tunnel of the vagina, lay in front of her as they drove.

At home she told George she had to go to the loo. In the bathroom she opened the book Devlin had given her. On the title page a telephone number had been scrawled. She flicked through the book and found the painting again. In this size and in photographic colour it had nothing of the impact of the seemingly living oil. She flushed the loo and returned to George.

George was inside her. His conscientious foreplay had not been necessary; when his finger finally journeyed down to her clitoris and along the slit of her vagina he found her wetter and hotter than she could ever remember being. (With George.) She lay on her back and pulled him into her. She wanted to be filled, to squeeze herself on a hard penis. When he was in her she closed her eyes and the painting returned. She felt the colours, the graduations of colour in her cunt. Her cunt was that red, that passionate crimson. Using her vaginal muscles she squeezed his penis. As he tried to push in and pull out she caught him inside and held him squeezing rhythmically stopping his withdrawal, using the rhythm of her cunt instead of the rhythm of his thrusts. She remembered Devlin looking at her while she looked at the painting. She remembered his hand on her breast. She remembered the older woman in the painting looking down at the other. She saw Devlin's face in detail. The incredibly bulbous nose with hair growing from the nostrils, the thick black wiry hair.

The wedge of his forehead projecting out over his eyes, the crest of the ridge grassed with black bushy eyebrows. His big fleshy loose mouth and irregular tombstone teeth.

She arched herself up against George, pushing her clitoris against the hard bone of his pelvis, squeezing on him harder and harder until there were no pauses between contractions, just continuous pressure as if her vaginal muscles had spasmed and locked around his penis. Her orgasm started in this muscle spreading outwards until she could feel it in every locked taut muscle, now into her thighs and knees, up into her abdomen, her arms, her neck. The feeling vibrated in the muscles as it poured out of her.

But it was over quickly. It left very little aftermath. The release was quick and absolute. She felt George begin to thrust up into her again and realised her vagina must have unlocked itself. She had certainly issued no orders to that effect. With the little energy she had left she helped him, moulded herself to his movement, twisted under him. She did not have the energy to reach down and take his balls in her hand. Sorry George. She did not feel him come, and did not want to, but she heard him groan and the thrusting stopped. He did not groan with much enthusiasm. Sorry George.

She watched him dress. He left, kissing her perfunctorily on the cheek as she nestled back into the bed. The duvet was warm and smelt of that sweet and sour smell of sex. She heard him slam the front door but was too comfortable to go and put the chain on. She could feel sleep was deliciously near, just out of reach.

So much for her controlled experiment. Devlin and the painting had so disturbed her, inflamed her, that by the time she got boring George to bed he was no longer boring, no longer George. She would have come whatever he had done, with no time for 'scientific' comparison.

Why hadn't she been outraged at Devlin's suggestion? Why had she not pushed his hand away from her breast instead of accepting the gesture as normal? She seemed to be attracting sexually-orientated experiences. Like a victim attracting the crime? Perhaps Devlin had sensed her mood, her preoccupation. Or perhaps he was used to the painting and the effect it had on women.

The telephone number in the book was like a hook in the mouth of a fish. She could feel the line tighten, imperceptibly at first. It would take some time before the reeling-in would bring her to the telephone. Then the line would slacken again and she would not dial. But sooner or later the nylon line would tighten fatally and she would dial and Devlin could pull her clear of the water and could have her in that bed facing the painting. As his small hairy body heaved itself into her she would open her eyes and see the trio of bodies held together by the orchid-like vulva.

And she had not thought of Martin all evening.

11

And Martin had not thought of her, it appeared. Stephanie did not see him for two weeks. Their paths did not cross and he made no attempt to phone her, either at work or at home. At first she thought it was coincidence but as the days passed she began to think he was deliberately avoiding her in the corridors and lifts of the building, hiding around corners, asking friends to see if the coast was clear. Schoolboy games of hide and seek.

Of course Martin was a stranger, and their intimacy did not make him any less so. She did not know him at all. She knew where he worked and where he lived. She knew what his voice sounded like and what he looked like naked, but that was all. She did not know how he behaved, reacted, thought. It was not possible for her to judge what he would do next in their relationship. He might regard her merely as a score, a notch on his metaphorical belt. His only interest might be to collect notches, and not to pursue them once collected. In that case, '*le weekend*' was a promise he had no intention of keeping.

That was one theory. But she did not actually believe it. It was extremely difficult to be objective about something as subjective as sex but, as she went over it in her mind, she decided that she did not believe that it had not been as special for him as it was for her. Sex was two people after all. It takes two. Martin had been there too. He had felt what she had felt. He had moved in the same way, been moved in the same way. It was not just a matter of technique, even bizarre technique.

She was absolutely clear about two things however. Firstly she had no sort of emotional attachment to Martin. His silence was not bothering her on that level. She did not even like him. Secondly, and equally clearly, she wanted him again. She wanted him again sexually. She did not want the sexual adventure to end so briefly.

It was that simple.

They were drunk. Not very drunk but drunk enough. Drunk enough for Joyce not to drive. They had called a taxi and now stood outside Joyce's house while she tried to find the keys in her voluminous handbag. It was a major undertaking. Things clattered on to the path and were ignored by both women. They stood in a pile of paper handkerchiefs, combs, a paperback Nietzsche, half a box of tampons which fell open side down spilling the contents, a bottle, now broken in all probability, of edible vitamin C tablets.

She made an attempt to pick some of the things up when Joyce had opened the door but Joyce insisted she left it all until the morning.

Joyce's house was small and pretty. It was what books on interior design would have called feminine. Cushions in pastel colours toned with the pastel coloured wallpapers and matching curtains. Little tables with table cloths draped to the floor. Flowers and flounces. Ornaments on every flat level surface. Books in neat shelves in neat alcoves.

Joyce poured them both brandy but did not offer coffee. They were too far gone for coffee. They drank the brandy in silence making themselves comfortable as the room began to warm up from the fire Joyce had lit.

She looked into the flames and sipped brandy. Though she felt slightly giddy it was not enough to dispel the general feeling of wellbeing that the evening with Joyce had created. The long intense chat over dinner in the local Italian. Everything from Mozart to menstruation, mildew to Marx, mice to men. She had told Joyce about Martin. And, as always with Joyce, had been told exactly what she wanted to hear.

'There's nothing wrong with sex, for God's sake. Nothing at all. My God, just enjoy it. Don't let it get to you. You've got a good healthy appetite, haven't you? If someone offers you a hearty meal you don't start asking if you really should eat it? You eat. You gorge. You compliment the chef like the nice well-brought up girl you are and say thank you very much. In the morning you can go on a diet. Well, it's the same with sex.'

Of course, Stephanie hadn't told her the whole story. She hadn't told her about her fascination with the books, or what had actually happened. In fact not telling her made it seem infinitely less important; put it into perspective. Behind closed doors, it was her secret. She watched the fire and Joyce watching the fire. They had first met when she moved to London. Joyce was one of the girls in the flat she had shared. £12.50 a week and all the bills divided into four except the telephone. All telephone calls had to be paid for by cash in the biscuit tin by the phone. Any tampering with the biscuit tin was punishable by instant dismissal from the flat, eternal ignominy, and the prospect of tramping the streets for another two weeks, *Evening Standard* in hand, looking for another flatshare. The biscuit tin was, therefore, generally inviolate.

But she did want to know whether Joyce had a secret. Whether her experience was shared.

'What are you thinking about?'
'Secrets?'
'What sort of secrets?'
'Fantasies.'
'They're not secret, are they?'
'Aren't they?'
'Mine aren't. I decided a long time ago I'd settle for half a million. A million is entirely unnecessary. Half a million would be quite enough.'
'Not that sort of fantasy.'
'Is there another sort?'
'Sexual.'
'Half a million is a sexual fantasy in the end. Not directly, but sex comes into it.'
'Pure sexual fantasy.'
'Like being tied up and raped?'

She could feel herself blush, blush deep red. She turned slightly in the hope that Joyce wouldn't notice. She appeared not to.

'Yes.'
Joyce laughed. 'Oh yes, they're secret.'
'But are they . . . real?'
'Fantasies can't be real.'
'But a lot of sex is fantasy isn't it? A lot of it just goes on inside the head.'
'Is this what he's done to you?'
'It's partly him.'
'Well.'

'He makes me feel different.'

'You said.'

'I don't just mean because he's so good at it. He makes me think things.'

'Things that turn you on? Like talking dirty?'

'Exactly. Except not talk. It's in my mind. It's nothing he says.'

She was getting close to the truth. She didn't mind telling Joyce the truth as part of an exchange, she decided, but she was not going to declare it unilaterally. She was not that drunk.

'Like sexual telepathy?'

'Yes. I've never experienced it before. It's not that he lives out my favourite sexual fantasy, some scenario I've always wanted to play, but he creates the fantasy . . . He makes me want it.'

'I know what you mean.'

'Do you?'

The golden stream.

'It happened to me once. It's marvellous at first. Intoxicating. Like a new strong drink you've never had before and you want again and again once you've got the taste for it. Until you think you can't live without it.'

'Breathtaking.'

Right. But it's not an addiction. It wears off. There's some mechanism, some little switch that one day, one day in the middle of it all, as you're coming with the earth moving on a Richter scale of ten, that little switch moves over to off and . . . well things change.'

'Change?'

'As you said. It's in the mind, isn't it? Well, suddenly the mind obviously decides to see things in a different way. The picture your mind was telling you five seconds before was the sexiest thing you'd ever seen becomes passé, boring, even sordid. It turns you off.'

'Why?'

'Don't ask me. That's what happened to me.'

'You think that'll happen to me?'

'I don't know. What I was involved in seems incredible to me now. How I could have done it? Why did I do it? I can think of every reason in the world why the whole thing was a terrible turn-off and I could say to myself I only agreed to it because I was in love or didn't know how to say no, or something. But that's not true. I wanted it too. He made me want it. It turned me on so much. I'd never had sex like it. If I'm really honest with myself that's the strict truth.'

'Your secret.'

'It's not a secret.'

Joyce had been out to dinner with Eric a few times. She'd even been to bed with him months before their affair started in earnest. That time it had been nothing special; she could hardly remember what happened. Just a few minutes coupled together, trying to find something, their bodies thrusting to find some common interest, some affinity, without success. But then, after a business dinner one night, Eric had given her a lift home. He told her he was desperate for a pee and asked if she would mind if he came in. The trouble was she was desperate too and there was only one toilet in her house. When she admitted the state of her bladder to him, assuming he would be the gentleman and let her go first his reaction was quite different. As she started upstairs he began to tease her, taunt her, stand in her way, stop her from getting to the loo. Instead of being cross she found herself laughing almost hysterically and playing the same game with him. Pulling him back, prodding at his bladder with her finger, pushing it with the flat of her hand. Her desire to pee was becoming uncontrollable and so was his. The laughter making it worse, uncontrollable.

Then it was too late to make it to the loo, too late to take off trousers, pants, raise skirts, take down knickers, and tights. Too late to do anything but stand together, hugged together, kissing deep long kisses, and feel the waves of relief as they gave into the overwhelming need and soaked their clothes and each other.

They had sex on the carpet, in the wet stain on the hall carpet, in their wet clothes, pulling them apart to gain access. Only her tights were removed through necessity but her knickers, as his, were only pushed aside, the soaking material pushed together against their bodies. They had come quickly, almost as soon as he entered her, but that had been enough for Joyce to reach a shattering climax as she felt his penis jerking inside her.

Eric was erect again almost immediately, growing hard inside her, never having slipped from her cunt. This time it was slower. They had time to pull away blouse and shirt. Time to kiss and caress before the rhythm of sex took over, before gentle, thoughtful, movement became hard urgent thrusts, before control became uncontrollable again, and words turned into thoughts, and thoughts became wild flying creatures filling the mind with electric sensation to which there seemed to be no end but the end, a final obliterating darkness.

After the first time, after he admitted it had always been something he had wanted to do – though he swore he'd never done it before – it became ritual. More hygienic, less expensive on dry-cleaning, but not less exciting. Joyce held him while he peed. Held him out. He knelt between her legs holding her labia open while she peed. If Eric were naked Joyce could see the surge this produced in the engorgement of his penis, the veins swelling and tight. They would rush to bed.

A rubber sheet was bought so they could lay together when their bladders were full — made deliberately full — and wait, kissing and caressing as the need increased, slowly, inexorably; resistible at first but increasingly irresistible until together they would decide and the first trickles would turn to a torrent.

He tried to pee while he was inside her. He had read it was possible but he was never able to do it. She peed over him lying naked on the rubber sheet: he peed on her.

'Does that shock you?'

'Of course not.' Stephanie was in no position to moralise.

'He didn't make me do it. I wanted to. It made me so hot.'

'I know the feeling. But you said it stopped.'

'As I said. No apparent reason. Nothing we hadn't done before, nothing he'd said. I just didn't want it any more.'

'Did you finish with him?'

'Not immediately. But he wanted to go on with it. It was the only way he wanted sex. I wanted . . . I wanted to get back to something . . . normal. He didn't. Couldn't. So we stopped having sex and that was all we'd ever had in common.'

The fire was roaring now. Joyce poured them another drink.

'It's sordid, isn't it?'

'No. It's what I was talking about. Martin said something the other night. Because we don't need sex any more, biologically need, we've got to invent something else, something to make it work again, stop us getting bored. Not just pleasure.'

'Might be better if we just forgot about sex.'

'More trouble than it's worth.'

'So tell me your secret.'

She told Joyce her secret and they agreed it was the same. The same experience. The same mechanism. The same psychological mechanism. Whatever that meant. Casebook study for the use of. They agreed there was nothing wrong with any of it, nothing perverted, nothing immoral, no eternal damnation if they had believed in eternal damnation. Good clean fun. They agreed it would end for her just as it had for Joyce, suddenly, another paragraph, section, chapter, ended. Another interest, affair, leitmotif would begin. She felt infinitely better for talking to Joyce and thanked God Martin had not wanted to pee on her.

It would end abruptly, without warning, as Joyce had said. But she had to admit to herself, though not to Joyce, that in her wildest dreams, her most fervent invention, she could not for the life of her imagine how.

Two days later the phone rang. It was Martin.

'Hello.'

'Hello.' She recognised his voice immediately.

'How are you?'

'Fine. You?'

'I've been busy.'

'Oh.'

'Are you free next weekend?'

He didn't ask whether she still wanted to. 'Yes.'

'I'll pick you up on Friday night.'

'Where are we going?'

'Away. Does it matter where?'

'No.'

'About eight. Is that all right?'

She wanted to tell him he shouldn't be so damn arrogant. He shouldn't take it for granted that after two weeks of silence he could pick up the phone and summon her to his presence whenever it suited him. She wanted to tell him what he could do with his weekend.

'Yes.'

'See you then.'

It was extraordinary to her that she felt as excited by this call and the prospect of seeing him again as she had the first time; none of her resentment at the way he had behaved affected that. He was an enigma which, of course, made him more, not less, interesting, a fact she was sure that he was well aware of.

12

The phone rang again. It was Devlin.
'Why didn't you call me?'
'I had nothing to say.'
'You found the number.'
'Very subtle.'
'Anyway I'm calling you.'
'What do you want?'

She knew exactly what Devlin wanted. She knew what almost every man she had ever met wanted from her. They wanted access to her body. They wanted her to lie down and open her legs and generally cooperate − or at least not interfere − while they pushed their penis into her until it ejaculated sperm. As it was that basic, that uncomplicated, she had never understood why men seemed to concentrate on beautiful women for the fulfilment of their desires. Why wouldn't any woman do? Was it that beauty helped them get up? Was it that taking a beautiful woman made them feel somehow better than taking an ugly or plain woman? Perhaps reinforced the poor battered male ego, like owning a beautiful painting, and knowing it was yours? Devlin had a very beautiful painting . . .

'To take you out to dinner.'

'I'm not available.'
'I see. Is there anything I can do to change your mind?'
'No.'
'I could beg.'
'That wouldn't be very dignified.'
'I thought you liked my painting.'
But I don't want to go to bed with you Mr Devlin.
'It is very beautiful.'
'Come and see it again, then.'
'I might.'
'Good.'
'I've got your number.'
'Please. Any time.'

Friday was four days away. She could not sleep. She lay in bed, her mind sub-vocalising conversations and imagined conversations, things she had said, things she should have said, things she would have liked to have said. Reams of dialogue as she lay with her eyes closed hoping that sleep would come and rescue her from her consciousness.

Conversations with Martin. What she should have said on the phone. What she was going to say when she saw him again. Where was he going to take her? What would he do?

Conversations with Joyce. What she'd said. Peeing together. Peeing together Behind closed doors. A different world, a world hidden by the neat public facade. In inverse proportion to the degree of neatness? The neater the facade the more extreme the sexual proclivities? Lying on a rubber sheet in a pool of steaming pee and fucking as hard, as hot, as she had with Martin while he had her tied and blindfolded. Was it the same?

Devlin. Conversations with Devlin while she stared

at the crimson vulva. While she described it to him as she stood in front of it naked and he kissed her, kissed her breasts, navel, thighs, parted her legs to kiss her clitoris, her oh-so pale clitoris in comparison with the blood-red colour there in front of her eyes. How he'd talked her into bed, how she'd looked into his grotesque face as he lay on top of her, entered her.

What would Martin do to her this time? The same? She had read in the books that sexual obsessions tended to deepen, become more intense. The fire needed continually more fuel or it would dwindle, and since fire was the point this could not be allowed to happen. A masochist who found he liked the taste of pain might start with a gentle pinch but gradually would need more and more until only the pain of an open wound would do; would he then need a large wound? And then the final pain? Is that what was going to happen to her? Would she want to progress up or down depending on your point of view — the scale of perversion? No, not perversion. Joyce had said it was not perversion; they had agreed on that.

Was Devlin's penis like his gargoyle's nose? Was it ridged and rutted, warted and veined? Would that turn her on? Would touching, sucking, fucking a grotesque penis turn her on? If it had not been for Martin there is no doubt that she would have phoned Devlin. There was no doubt she would have wanted Devlin. Perhaps Devlin could provide her with a diversion to make the time go more quickly. Time was on her hands until Friday. She did not want to spend the next four days waiting, speculating, thinking about Martin. An evening with Devlin would pass the time. She didn't have to go to bed with him after all.

The phone interrupted her train of thought. It was Joyce. She sounded unsettled, if not anguished.

'What's the matter, Joyce?'
'It's been worrying me.'
'What?'
'The other night . . .'
'What?'
'I shouldn't have told you . . .'
'Why on earth not?'
'I had a lot to drink. I didn't mean to.'
'Don't be silly. We're old friends, aren't we?'
'That's what I mean. I don't want it to affect . . . I don't want you to think I'm . . .'
'I don't think anything. Is it any worse than what I told you?'
'I don't know. It won't change anything, will it?'
'Joyce.'
'It's been on my mind that's all. I know it's silly.'
'It is. Forget it. I certainly will.'

Sounding not at all reassured Joyce rang off. It seemed strange she thought, that Joyce should be so concerned at her image in the eyes of such an old friend. She hadn't felt the drink had been responsible for revelation. She had felt so much better about her own position as a result of the conversation, and surely that was what friends were for. It had never occurred to her to question Joyce's behaviour or to think any less of her because of it. Obviously Joyce felt differently. Sexual confession was not good for the soul.

Unless it was guilt by association. Joyce was worrying about what her friend would think of her precisely because she had been shocked at her friend's disclosures. An amity of guilt. Unplumbed depths. Murky waters. Well it would either bring them closer together, or it wouldn't and there was nothing she could do about it now.

Stephanie took out one of the books. (She thought

of them as The Books.) Unplumbed depths indeed. She opened it at random, skipping the endless pseudo-psychological commentary until she got to an extract supposedly from some pornographic epic:

> The black latex suit fitted skin-tight, covering his body, feet and hands to his neck, like a wet suit except the suit only had one leg into which both his limbs were crammed. A rubber hood was pulled over his head. The last 'white' of flesh disappeared. Black rubber man. The hood had no eye or ear holes; two small openings over the nostrils to allow him to breath were the only breaks in the solid rubber.
>
> Thick rubber straps bound his arms to his sides at the waist and across the chest. He was now placed in another rubber cover that zipped up to enclose him completely. Two small tubes were passed through this cover and into his nostrils. The cover was then inflated with a small air-bed pump. As the air filled the bag it became a great rubber ball, two little tubes protruding from the top.
>
> The pump was hard work. The two girls alternated the effort between them until the job was completed.
>
> A bouncing black rubber ball. Rubber Ball Man. Engulfed in the feel and smell of rubber. One of the girls kicked the ball and it bounced around the room.

It was Wednesday night. She was reading again when the phone rang. George had a cold. He didn't want to go out. He didn't want her to come round and nurse him. He just wanted to be left alone to die in peace. He was terribly sorry.

It didn't cross her mind for a moment that he was not telling the truth, even though he didn't sound particularly ill. George was too simple to lie. Still she was mildly annoyed with him; good old reliable George wasn't being very reliable. She had needed him tonight. She had wanted the distraction. If she thought about it she wasn't exactly sure if distraction was the only reason. She could manage George, control him. Most of her adult life she had been in control, she had made the decisions, taken the choices. Now, temporarily, that had changed. That was part of the excitement, of course. But George, good old reliable George, was a reminder of what things were like under normal circumstances.

Was he the last vestige of that life or would normal service be resumed and her control return? She did not know. Nor, interestingly enough, did she know which she would prefer. Not that she had any choice as she was not in control. Such thoughts were purely idle. In fact she did not want to think of the future. She did not want to think of next weekend, of next week or next month. She did not want to think what lay beyond her current preoccupation.

Of course Devlin beckoned her now. Devlin. His beautiful house, his beautiful paintings, his esoteric attraction. The other night she had felt herself perfectly capable of resisting the temptation. Now tonight she was considerably less sure.

She picked up the book again. She had bought it at lunch time. She had always been quite blatant about going into what had become known as sex shops – though the very last thing they sold was sex – despite the fact she was always the only woman. At first she had to admit she enjoyed it. Not because of any sexual thrill, it was not playing the tease, but because of the reactions she provoked among the other patrons. Men browsing among the explicitly illustrated magazines and badly printed books, far from overtly or furtively eyeing her up and down, looked away, pulled themselves in, tried to make themselves as small as possible, like hedgehogs rolling themselves into a ball. As if, as a representative of womankind brave and free, she came to chastise them, releasing their guilts and fears. The women in the magazines, their pouting vulvas, their massive tits, their whipped buttocks or tightly bound arms, come to life to worry and harry their tormentors. Harpies of the Muse of Pornography. Well, one harpy.

She never thought that it was a dangerous game to play. She never imagined her presence would provoke more than guilt and fear, would create anger, resentment and violence. Was that her naivety or just the truth?

The heavy who sat behind the counter, apparently having great difficulty reading the *Sun*, did not like her either. She was bad for business. The men left quickly, in their coats of prickles, and very few dared to buy anything while she was in the shop. He had not said anything to her but his grunts were expression enough. His grunts were language enough. A grunt for 'not you again', a grunt for 'get on with it then, make it quick for God's sake', a short high-pitched grunt for 'you shouldn't be here'.

After a while the novelty wore off. She looked on it as a rather bizarre library. She ignored the men. She would have looked them straight in the eye except not one man had ever met her gaze. She went to the books and browsed. Mostly, she had learned, the books with the most lurid covers were the least interesting. Interesting was a euphemism for obscene, pornographic, explicit. The most explicit books usually had plain covers with simple graphic titles – *Bound in Chains, Dominatrix, Rubber Slave, TV Fun*. The titles with slightly less overt meaning were occupied by crude pen and ink drawings of figures, their feet, hands, elbows and knees revealing the artist's distinct lack of ability, arranged in the position appropriate to the subject of the book. *Angela's Pleasure* with a drawing of a man on his knees kissing the foot of a woman in black stockings and corselet. *Rita and Susie*, with two women locked, naked in each other's arms.

At first she had no idea what attracted her to a particular book. She bought at random — given that random in such matters is accepted as being the product of some deep subconscious reflex. But now she was drawn to books on subjugation, bondage, domination. It fascinated her that the coin seemed to have two exactly equal and reverse sides. Sadism and masochism, domination and slavery. Often, in the books, the sadist would become the masochist, the dominator become the slave. It could have been that the authors were merely trying to cram in the maximum titillation and couldn't be bothered to introduce a new character. They just changed the traits of the old one and carried on hoping nobody would notice. But she felt there was actually a truth in it all. The slave did cry out to dominate, the sadist to become the victim. Taking it in turns. Her turn and his turn. Two exactly equal and opposite sides.

After all that was what had happened to her. That was what Martin had done to her, taught her: the game they'd played.

She put the book down. None of the words were registering. Devlin. Devlin. Damn George.

The phone rang twice before he answered, catching her by surprise.

'Oh, Mr Devlin?'

'Yes.' His voice sounded different.

'Is that Mr Devlin?'

'Hello. How are you? I'm glad you called.'

'You recognise . . .'

'You have a very distinctive voice. Are you coming over or do you want me to take you out?'

'You're very direct.'

'Isn't that why you're calling?'

'Yes.' There was no pointing in making up some complicated story.

'Which would you prefer, then?'

'Sorry?'

'Would you like me to take you out or would you rather come here?'

She didn't know what to say. He had succeeded in wrong-footing her completely.

'I tell you what,' he was making the decision for her, 'I'll come and pick you up. Then if you want to go and eat . . .'

'Lovely. Thank you.'

He was going to pick her up in an hour. She bathed quickly and dried herself energetically. In the bedroom she picked the matching beige bra and panties and decided against stockings. Too obvious for Devlin. (Did that imply she had already decided she was going to bed with him? Yes, but a girl can change her mind.) She had some very sheer black tights that went with the red dress and red high heels she was going to wear. In fact she was ready with fifteen minutes to spare.

13

He was exactly on time. As the clock struck nine. He declined the offered drink and led her to his car. It was large and foreign and the interior was leather and filled with blinking coloured lights and banks of switches and dials. She had no interest in cars, never had had, and Devlin made no attempt to mention anything about it. The seat was wonderfully comfortable and the car glided noiselessly along as Devlin drove. He drove straight to his house without asking her if she wanted dinner. The ride made her feel soporific. The cassette deck was playing Mozart. He did not talk, concentrating on his driving. She had no desire to talk to him. She was wallowing in a sudden and exhilarating sense of freedom.

The journey seemed to take no time at all. He got out of the car and walked round to open the car door for her. A perfect gentleman. Unlocking the front door of the house, he ushered her in.

'A drink? Are you hungry?'

'No, not really.'

'There's champagne. Or something stronger.'

In the living room she sank into one of the large sofas while he went to get the champagne. She didn't think she had ever been in a room so tastefully decorated. All the paintings were special, all the furniture perfect. No compromises. Enough money to make compromise unnecessary. He returned with a bottle of vintage champagne in a silver cooler on a tray with two crystal flutes. He opened the bottle and with practised ease poured without allowing the glasses to overfill. For a second she thought she was in an elaborate 1940's Hollywood movie except he definitely did not look like Cary Grant.

As he handed her the glass she noticed his hands. He had the most enormous fingers she had ever seen. Each was the size of a banana and that was no exaggeration. The fingernails were each as big as a fifty-pence piece. His whole hand looked like a bunch of bananas, four large curved ones and a smaller withered cousin hiding at the side. The sexual implications did not dawn on her for a moment until she suddenly imagined what it would be like to have one of those inside you. It would have to be one, two would be quite impossible. (Nothing's impossible.) One would be as big as some penises.

If he saw her staring he made no comment, nor did he attempt to hide his hands away. She noticed that despite their size his use of them was deft.

'Why did you phone?'

'I was bored.'

'Not very complimentary.'

'I wanted a preoccupation.'

'To take your mind off what.'

That was sharp. 'What do you mean?'

'Preoccupations usually mean something is being avoided.'

'Do they?' She had no intention of talking about Martin to Devlin.

'Obviously not. How is George?'

'He has a cold.'

'Ah . . .'

'You're not a substitute for George I assure you.' There was a peculiar truth in that statement but she hoped she did not have to explain it.

'Why is that? Because George is not a player or because I am not a player?'

'I don't understand.'

'It was the way you said it. Either dismissive of me or dismissive of George.'

'You don't let anything past, do you?'

'Language is my specialty. It fascinates me. Simple sentences can convey the most complex thoughts. Intonation. Inflection. Resonance. A word can have twenty meanings, can't it?'

'Depending on how it is said.'

'Exactly. My theory is that the more complex the subject the word represents, the more meanings it can have in conversations. But funnily enough the word has got to be simple in itself. Words like pernicious, animalistic, grandiose . . .'

'Elephantine . . .?' He did not react to the unfortunate choice.

'They don't really have verbal ambiguity. But short simple words. Home. Safe. Love, Brave. Free. Sex. They can be said in such a way as to mean a hundred different things.'

'"Love" is certainly loaded.'

'Are you in love with George?'

'No.'

'What then?'

'I might not want to answer that.'

'Do you like him?'

'No.' She said it too quickly, an automatic response. 'He's all right.'

'Keeps you occupied.'

'Why are you so curious about me.'

'You know you're a very beautiful woman?'

'I have been told.'

'For many years I suspect. Though to do you credit I don't know that you entirely believe it. Anyway I want to know the genealogy of beauty.'

'That, not a subject that interests me very much.'

He led her on. At first she was aware that they had been talking for an hour or so. But then the time disappeared as he led her through the story of her life. He was attentive and appeared to be totally fascinated. Always asked the right question at the right moment. Always led her from one dead end to the next open road with exactly the right reference to what she had been saying moments before. Any attempts she had made earlier to hold back, to self-censure remarks, had gone. As the evening progressed she was telling him everything. The boy in the darkened room, his two fingers up her hot wet cunt. All the stories. Betraying her friend Joyce – my friend actually did it with a man who wanted to pee all over her, and she really liked it, got hot for it – and telling Penny's sad story too. But she did not mention Martin.

It was late.

'George isn't the only man in your life, is he?' He didn't miss a thing.

'No.'

'Who, then?'

'A man at work.' Devlin sensed the iron shutter descend with a decisive clatter and stopped immediately. The champagne was long gone. He had made coffee while she had followed him into the kitchen still talking, but that was finished too. She felt dehydrated and a little drunk. For her, drunkenness was always betokened by a feeling of detachment from her body; of seeing herself sitting on the sofa looking at Devlin from the viewpoint of the ceiling above.

'Do you want to go home?'

'No.'

'Do you want to go to bed?'

'No.'

'It's very late.'

'You said bed meaning sex.'

'Not necessarily.'

She was sharp, bright and sharp. 'Not necessarily meaning that I could go to bed here without you or that we could have sex without going to bed?'

'Logical positivism at this hour.'

'You didn't answer.'

'Both.'

'Which?'

'Whichever you please.'

'Don't you have any preference?'

'Yes.'

'Do I have to drag it out of you?'

'I would like to take you to bed and make love.'

'Ah.'

'Is that possible?'

'No.'

'O.K. Then . . .'

'You give up easily.'

'Rape is a criminal offence.'

'There is an alternative.'

'What?'

'What *I* want.' She did not want to go upstairs with him. To stare into the crimson vulva as she felt many women had done while he fucked them. She had thought she would want that very much, thought it

133

would be a terrific turn-on. But at this moment the idea appalled her. And she wanted something else.

Devlin did not move when she got up. She stood and pulled her dress over her head.

She kissed him on the mouth, feeling the enormous nose, feeling his banana fingers rise to cup her head and pull it on to his mouth. The touch of his hand, the touch of those gigantic fingers made her feel excited, suddenly wildly excited. She kissed him harder, finding his other hand with hers and interlocking her fingers with his. Her fingers could hardly protrude through the width of his. Her hand felt dainty, tiny, like a Japanese, like one of George's tiny Japanese women who bowed and scraped to him. Devlin broke from the embrace and got up. He turned most of the lights out and dimmed the remainder until the room was bathed in an eerie grey light. He began to unbutton his shirt. She reached behind her and unclipped her bra. From the ceiling she watched herself as her breasts swung free. She watched Devlin. For a second, before image regained its hold, he looked like a child at an amusement arcade who has actually won the enormous cuddly toy. She sensed for the first time an inexperience and uncertainty. Then the more droll expression returned. She sat back on the sofa in knickers and tights.

He stood in front of her and took off his shirt and socks – shoes had long been abandoned. She smiled from the ceiling at the manoeuvre – another *Cosmopolitan* reader. Dropping to her knees in front of him, she undid his belt and pulled his trousers and pants down in one movement. His penis was flaccid, his pubic hair copious and very dark. As with his face, hair grew everywhere on his body, clumps and forests of thick wiry hair on his back, shoulders, thighs, navel.

Gorilla Man. He stepped out of the trousers as she resumed her position on the sofa.

Now he knelt in front of her naked. He kissed her knees. She parted her legs allowing him to kiss inside her knee and thigh. He kissed her cunt hidden under tights and knickers. He took the tights in his hands and pulled down. She cooperated by lifting her bum. He caught the knickers too on the way down and pulled tights and knickers free of her legs. Repeating his performance he kissed her knee again and again as she parted her legs for him; he kissed along the inside of her thigh until he reached her now naked cunt. His tongue flicked at her clitoris. He had found it so accurately that she could not suppress a moan. He flicked at it again, working on it, sucking it, pushing it from one side to the other with his tongue.

She felt his hand holding her thigh. The image of those fingers so close to her open cunt made her feel hot. His hand got closer nearer to the opening. He sensed what she wanted. Maybe it was what every woman he had wanted, what fascinated them, what they really wanted from him. His tongue flicked at her again but now she could feel his hand under his mouth, feel his forefinger prod her dark opening and enter, and push up and up and fill her, round and hard, like a penis but harder than a penis, much harder. Warm and hard. At first he was content to leave it up inside her as he concentrated on her clitoris, but she was not. She began to squirm on it. Ride on it. Lift herself away from it and then push down again. Squirm and ride. Squirm until he could not keep his mouth on her, until he moved his mouth to her nipple and she could wriggle down on his finger freely.

She felt herself coming from a long way back. She could feel it building. In her mind she wondered if she could take another finger. She could feel the rest of his fist curled up there outside her cunt, at the lips of her cunt. Would he try to force another one in? The idea was planted in her mind. Every movement of his hand made it grow, blossom and grow; just as her orgasm was blossoming and growing. She thought she felt a fingernail begin to push the soft flesh aside, she thought she felt the elasticity of her cunt begin to stretch . . . But then the waves of orgasm overcame her and it didn't matter what he was doing for the idea had been enough and she sobbed and shuddered and moaned in delight.

He extracted his finger from her gently and lay on the sofa beside her. She kissed him, letting her hand run down his body until she found his lap. He was still flaccid. Without wanting to be obvious she ran her hand over his navel and the tops of his thighs. Had he come as she came? Apparently not.

The view from the ceiling, she realised, had disappeared. Her point of view was entirely normal again.

Moving her head she kissed his neck and his chest through the mat of hair. She took his nipple in her mouth and bit it quite hard. He did not moan. Her hand encircled his penis, wanking it slowly, feeling for any stirring as she kissed him. Slowly she descended until her head was in his lap. Using her hand she guided his penis into her mouth. She sucked at it, pulled at it by moving her head away, nudged it inside her mouth with her tongue. She squeezed his balls with her hand. She lifted his penis with her hand and took one of his balls in her mouth. None of these party pieces produced the slightest stirring.

Was he Rubber Man, Leather Man, Schoolgirl Uniform Man? An object lesson from the pages of pornographic literature. What was his secret? *Dear Forum, I am unable to obtain an erection unless I am first allowed to wear the knickers of my sweetheart. If her knickers are particularly dirty my erection is truly a wonder to behold. Unfortunately none of the women I have met really understands my needs and are indeed horrified by it. Can anything be done for me?* Editor: *You could go to work in a laundry.*

'What can I do? Is it me?'

'No. No, it isn't.'

'Is there something you want me to do?'

'Come upstairs to the bedroom. Please.'

The painting. The crimson vulva would be in her line of vision from the bed. So simple. *Dear Forum, I can only get it up if I can see my favourite painting while I'm doing it.* Stephanie got up and walked upstairs without a word. In the bedroom she stood in front of the painting as she had with George beside her. The vulva was not as she had remembered it. It was brighter, more alive, more open, more suggestive, more erotic. It made her feel somehow inadequate, less than passionate. She leant forward slightly so she was closer to it. It looked so alive she felt it would move. So wet and hot she felt she would feel the warmth, the smell.

Devlin came into her from behind. Her cunt was still wet — or had become wet again — but the surprise of feeling his hot penis push into her made her cry out. He had wrapped his arms around her waist, pulling her back into him, her buttocks into his navel. She wanted to splay her arms out in front of her for balance but she could not rest her hands on the oil of the painting. His penis was filling her, but as she felt him push up she realised that only the tip was inside her. He was massive. She reached down between her legs and felt for him. She could feel him at the top of her womb and yet there was still inches of him outside her, pushing up into her, trying to sheath himself in her. There was no more room. She turned to try to see his face but could not. She wanted to tell him she could take no more of him but at the same time wanted to see if she could. My God, it was the same as his fingers! Could she take more? Almost as it occurred to her she felt the orgasm beginning. He was not moving in her. The only slight movement from him was upward gradually feeding more and more of himself into her. But she didn't want it to be gradual now. She started to move on him as she had on his fingers. Pushing herself back and down on him. Feeling the neck of her womb push up into her under the pressure of his penis, feeling the mouth of her cunt stretch, seeing in her mind's eye the ring of flesh stretched white by him. She rolled her hips and pushed down once more until the orgasm made her forget everything, all incentive to move, wiped everything away but itself until it too had gone and she found herself so weak she could hardly stand up against him.

He took her over to the bed and laid her down. She looked to one side to see what had penetrated her. He was enormous. Nose, fingers, penis. The old jokes were true. Like a mule. Hung like a mule. But he was. How could she have accommodated that? She couldn't have taken more than a quarter.

'Will you come?' She wasn't sure how she wanted him to answer.

'Yes.'

'In me?'

'Will you let me do what I want?'

'Yes.'

It was his turn.

He knelt on the bed between her thighs. At first she

thought he was going to lower himself on her, penetrate her again. She braced herself. Now she had actually seen him she could not help but worry. But he had no intention of entering her again. He took his penis in his hand and began to wank very slowly and deliberately. His other hand reached out and touched her nipple, just the lightest touch as though to reassure himself she was real, then it wandered back and down between her legs until it rested on her clitoris, the slightest of pressures. His fist being so large, it held a lot of his penis. A normal hand, her hand, would barely have grasped the top. As he wanked she watched the tube of his penis. It was gnarled like a knotted piece of wood, the veins seemingly clotted into tight knots of blood. She watched as the precursory tear developed from the eye and was enveloped by his hand. She watched as he glanced over his shoulder at the painting – a surreptitious look. She watched as his hand movements got faster, his penis harder; she watched as he moaned very softly and a thick cream of sperm brimmed over his hand and down over his fingers.

He rocked back slightly on his heels. His finger left her clitoris. Reaching out he took tissues from the bedside table and wiped his hand. Carefully he moved from over her and lay by her side. There was a small spot of his sperm on her navel. He took another tissue and delicately, like trying to remove a spot of paint so the stain wouldn't spread, dabbed it off.

Stephanie dozed off. He lay beside her, his body touching her. His eyes closed. She thought she'd just doze off for a few minutes then get up and go home. The bedroom was warm and she couldn't be bothered to get into the bed to cover her naked body. As she closed her eyes the crimson vulva smiled at her, a wide grinning smile. She smiled back. It winked at her but she was too tired to wink back and closed her eyes, feeling the numbness of sleep at the edges of her mind almost immediately.

When she woke light streamed through the gaps in the curtains. The bedside clock told her it was six. He had gone. She looked round for her clothes then remembered they were all downstairs. For a moment she debated going back to sleep and going into work without going home first. No, she couldn't face that. She got up and went into the bathroom. She peed and then wrapped herself in a towel.

He was in the kitchen fully dressed. The coffee was made and an ice-cold glass of orange juice sat on the table. She gulped down the juice but refused the offer of anything else for breakfast. The hot coffee after the cold orange was lovely.

He had picked up her clothes and folded them neatly on the kitchen table. She began to dress. He asked her if she'd prefer him to leave. After what had happened the night before that would have seemed ridiculous to her, but she still felt awkward as she dressed. She pulled her knickers on under the towel and then abandoned any attempt at modesty. How silly. She pulled the towel away and proceeded to dress, trying to ignore his presence. He watched her. He didn't take his eyes off her for one second as far as she could tell. Not that it will have given him a hard-on, she thought cynically. Perhaps if she'd rouged the lips of her cunt, rouged them crimson red . . .

He drove her home. Lack of sleep made her feel oddly alert, the extra effort needed to concentrate on being awake.

'Do you mind if I ask a personal question?'
'I can guess.'

'Well . . .?'

'The painting?'

'Yes. Do all your women ask.'

'I don't go to bed with many women.'

'But the ones you do?'

'Comment on the peculiarity? Yes.'

'Who is she?'

'Who?'

'The woman in the painting. Is it someone you know?'

'A portrait? Yes.'

'And she turns you on?'

'It's more . . . I never went to bed with her. I never saw her naked. I only knew her . . . socially.'

'Look, you don't have to tell me.'

'It's perfectly all right. She went to live in America. I discovered she had modelled for some paintings. There's one or two others of her in the house. I bought them all.'

'Were you in love with her?'

'No, I don't think so.'

'What then?'

'I don't know. I just don't know. It happened. The painting became . . . important . . . all important.'

There didn't seem to be much else he wanted to say and she could not think of anything else to ask. One of the strange things about casual one night stands was that though there is every appearance of the most personal intimacy in fact there is no intimacy at all. Sex had produced no insights, no breaking of barriers, established no rapports. He was a stranger to her, as much a stranger now as he had been before he had sat between her thighs and wanked himself off.

They reached her flat.

'I'd genuinely like to see you again.' He looked at

her sadly as he said it, as though he suspected she would genuinely never want to see him again.

'I'll call you next week.' Next week was, after all, a life time away, but Devlin did not know that and looked pleased. He kissed her on the cheek, got back into his car and drove away.

14

Thursday night and her case was neatly packed. She was taking too much but that was Martin's fault. An outfit for any occasion, a pair of shoes to go with an outfit for any occasion. The small weekend case had grown to a medium sized case. She didn't close the lid as she didn't want the clothes to crease.

Knowing it must be at least nine-thirty she looked at her watch. It was eight. Eight! Four more hours before she could decently go to bed. What on earth was she going to do? Ring George?

He still didn't sound ill but he said he felt it. He still didn't want company.

Joyce? She could see Joyce. There was no reply. Penny? Even Penny would do.

'Hello.'

'Are you up to anything this evening?'

'Nothing particular, why?'

Suddenly she was not sure she wanted to see Penny at all. More tearful stories of betrayal. 'Thought we could have a drink or something.'

'Great. Better still, come and share my casserole. There's more than enough for two.'

She got home at eleven-thirty. By the time she had

undressed and taken off her make-up it was midnight. She went to bed.

Sleep did not arrive. She lay in the dark, her mind alert and active. Penny had talked and talked and talked. It did occur to her that Penny was not entirely an innocent party when men walked out on her and generally treated her badly as they invariably seemed to do. The man who had refused to be seen out with her and scurried home immediately after the act might have done so not because he was ashamed at the way she looked but because he didn't want to inflict her on his friends.

That was not fair. Penny was a good friend. Loyal. Helpful. Supportive. Friends didn't have to be perfect. If she was a seamless chatterer it was a small price to pay for knowing she was there.

She looked at the bedside clock. Twelve-fifteen. The digits on the L.C.D. display changed to sixteen as she watched. She continued to watch, measuring in her mind how long a minute would be. At least five minutes later the digits flashed to seventeen. She closed her eyes again.

Friday tomorrow. Him tomorrow. His body, his face, his mind. Standing in her doorway with that slight smile. Sitting beside him as he drove. Watching him in profile as he drove. Unsmiling.

And then what? Checking into a hotel? Tied to the bed in a strange hotel bedroom? Then down to dinner before the restaurant closed: the happy couple. The happy couple in a dining room full of geriatrics; a seaside hotel full of wealthy old ladies waiting to die. All chuckling and whispering at the sudden appearance of young blood in their midst, the sudden appearance of sex among them reviving memories of what had been for them and what might have been.

As she would remember one day? As she would in her dotage remember this weekend? Remember what he did to her and what she did to him. Remember the purity of sex removed from any sort of personal relationship?

That thought alarmed her. It was something that hadn't occurred to her before. The times she had spent with him before had been brief. They had done nothing but make love. At his house she hadn't wanted to stay with him. She'd left as soon as the passion was spent. But she couldn't do that this weekend. She was stuck with him and illness wouldn't help her this time. What on earth were they going to talk about? They could hardly spend the whole time in sexually-related activities and their immediate aftermath.

It was true they had had lunch together. As she remembered, he had done most of the talking and she most of the listening. Apart from the fact that she was infatuated with him she had been rather bored. The performance had been too polished. It had been a performance. And, to be fair, so was the quiet, reserved manner she had adopted. Two images sitting down to lunch, not two people.

So what would the images be over dinner, Saturday breakfast, lunch and dinner, Sunday breakfast and lunch. An awful lot of suave sophisticated chatter, an awful lot of carefully chosen apt responses. An awfully long time to project the image.

And without the image? Would the boredom show? Did it matter? Was it possible that everything else but what they had in bed together was totally irrelevant and nothing to do with anything? What mattered was in their bed. In their bed and in their minds.

In one of those slick glossy executive woman's magazines actually read by women whose claim to being executive was as dubious as the magazine's claim to speak for them, she had read that women felt the main difference between men and women sexually was that a man was prepared to indulge in sex without precondition (a man would fuck anything with a pulse) but a woman had to have a whole list of prerequisites including the ability to communicate verbally with her proposed partner. Before Martin she had felt this more or less.

But that was before. Now, quite honestly, she could not give a damn. Liberation at last. She smiled at herself in the dark.

It would be interesting to see if this was a lasting development, a new pattern. She had after all approached him. She had taken the male role. To his credit he had not seemed to mind in the least. Other men might. On the other hand was it actually ever going to happen again? Was she ever going to feel again what she had felt for Martin, what Martin had aroused in her then and subsequently? She doubted it. If she did, she would know what to do.

Question. Given a feeling of overwhelming sexual attraction to a member of the opposite sex would you take the initiative and proposition them if a) you had never seen them before in your life, b) you knew them socially or through work, c) you knew them well and had done for some time. Your sexual Boldness Rating scores twenty if the answer to a) is yes, fifteen if the answer to b) is yes, and five if the answer to c) is yes. Score double if you are a woman.

She opened her eyes. The room was no longer dark. The light from the street seeping into the room from every unshielded cranny cast deep shadows, made strange shapes. She still felt no tiredness though her eyes felt sore and overused. Lying perfectly still she decided she was being silly and it was time to go to sleep. No thoughts. Clear mind. Relax.

Devlin. No, a clear mind. Think black or white. Think pure sheets of white. Stop thinking about thinking white. Just the white alone. On her own. No white. Cream getting white. Bleaching white. The washing will have to wait until next week. No white. White.

She concentrated again trying to feel her eyelids, trying to make her eyelids feel heavy. A sheet of white under her eyelids. Looking for sleep. Searching for it.

She turned the light on and picked up a book. (Mental note: take The Books off her bedside table before George's next visit.) Another extract.

They had her in every way two men can take one woman. They had both come in her cunt. They had come in her hair, over her face. She had sucked them, wanked them, fucked them. Her white body was covered with long red marks, marks of fingers dragged over her, pushed into her, clinging on to her. Marks of teeth biting her, lips kissing her. Marks of stubbled chins rubbed on her.

They were erect again. The one whose penis the woman had smeared with Vaseline lay on the bed on his back. The woman came and sat in his lap facing his feet. Reaching behind her she found his penis and slowly guided it to her arsehole. She rose on her haunches and lowered herself again until he was firmly and deeply embedded in her arse. The man reached out his hands and found her tits, cupping them in his palms and pulling her backward on to him, his fingers pinching at her nipples. Her fingers went to her cunt now, feeling her labia, holding it open for the other man who stood ready.

He knelt between the two sets of legs and put his penis between her cunt lips. He pushed home.

The woman gasped. Two men inside her. Two penises together inside her. A human sandwich. A cunt sandwich.

In the morning Stephanie overslept and woke up in a panic. She had not slept for long though. Black crescent moons adorned her eyes. Even extra make-up could not hide the damage. And she was too late to take the time to do her make-up properly anyway. God, she felt terrible. And not the chance of any sleep between now and tonight. Great. The stuff dreams are made of. Falling asleep over dinner. Falling asleep in bed.

If she left the office early she could try to get some sleep at home before he arrived. An hour would help. Leave at five. Home by six. Wake at seven. Even seven-fifteen. She'd still have time to dress and make-up. Plenty of time. Thank God she'd packed on Thursday night.

The thought of an hour's sleep got her through the day. She left the office at ten to five, running. Running to the tube. It was crowded. She stood all the way. Running from the tube to home. Home by five forty-five. Five forty-five as she closed her front door and looked at her watch. So she could sleep for an hour and a half, a whole hour and a half if she wanted to. Kicking off her shoes she went into the bedroom and lay on the bed. She unfastened her trousers and pulled the counterpane over her. With the anxiety of the day, the tiring journey home and lack of sleep she was tired and her eyelids felt heavy.

She slept. Not black unconscious sleep but sleep nevertheless. Sleep full of incident, images, half-truths, half dreams; that hinterland of sleep infused with reality but definitely not real.

Martin was early. Very early. She wasn't dressed, just dried from her bath. Pulling on a towelling robe she opened the door to him. He didn't smile, and said hello very curtly. As she turned to go back into the bedroom he caught the lapel of the robe to stop her. He kissed her on the mouth and opened the robe. He looked at her naked body, pink from the bath, as he held the robe open like the wings of a butterfly ready to be pinned. As she turned to go back into the bedroom he asked if he could help himself to a drink. She heard him pour it as she took off the robe and clipped on her bra. He came into the bedroom, drink in hand. She stepped into her knickers, black knickers to match the bra, but as she pulled them up over her thighs he hooked a finger into the waistband, preventing her pulling them up over her bum. She turned to face him her pubic hair half covered by the knickers. He sipped at his glass as she pulled her knickers on and fastened the suspenders, black to match her knickers and bra, threading the suspenders under the knickers. He told her, uncharacteristically, she thought, that she had beautiful breasts. She told him it was a flattering bra, which it was. She had chosen it specially to support her large breasts, hold them and push them into a deep cleavage. He kissed her cleavage, his tongue moving down between her breasts leaving a wet trail of saliva as his hand rubbed the soft black silk against her nipple. She could feel his erection against her navel. Martin held her head in his hands. She ran her hand over the front of his trousers and feeling his erection started to pull on the zip of his fly. But he turned away. Turned his back on her. He unzipped his trousers and let them drop with his pants to his knees. His bum looked tight and clenched. She wanted to kiss him, suck him, take him in her mouth, but he turned and she realised she could not. It was too big, his penis was too big. It was enormous. She could never get it into her mouth. She knew that because it was Devlin's penis.

15

Ten past seven and Stephanie woke feeling rested, the dream forgotten. She decided against having a drink in case it made her sleepy again. She ran a bath making it as hot as she could stand and drank a cup of tea as she lay in it. Then she scrubbed herself vigorously and dried herself with equal energy. Seven-thirty. It was a warm evening and she did not bother to put on her robe as she sat down to make-up. In the mirror her breasts were pink from the hot water, her shoulders even redder where she had scrubbed. By the time she had done her eyes, liner, a light shadow, a light mascara, the pink and red had faded.

She took her left breast in her hand. The nipple was flaccid and even when she flicked at it with her nail, showed no sign of arousal. Standing up she ran her hand down over her pubic hair and over her clitoris and labia.

In the bedroom she clipped on her bra. She had laid all the underwear out the night before. Only the grey stockings she had chosen to go with her black dress took any time to smooth into place so they did not wrinkle around the ankles or were too loose on the suspenders. She had learnt her lesson with stockings.

Satisfied she slipped into high heels and brushed her hair vigorously before pulling the dress over her head. Another final brush of the hair. Ten to eight.

The phone rang.

He was sorry he couldn't make it. He was sorry it had all been a terrible mistake. He should never have let it go so far. He was sure she'd understand. Better stop now before someone gets hurt.

'Hello.'

It was George. Today he sounded terrible.

'You sound terrible,' she said.

'I've been ill, remember?'

'You didn't sound ill before.' She desperately didn't want to be on the phone when Martin knocked at the door.

'I was.' He sounded hurt at the suggestion he might have been putting it on.

'I know, George. You told me.' Very sharp. Unpleasant.

'Are you all right?'

'Yes.'

'You don't sound it.'

'I'm, ah . . .'

'I could do with a visitor.'

'You said you were too ill for visits.'

'I'm feeling better.'

'You sound worse.'

'I know, but I feel better.'

'I can't this weekend, George.' She expected to hear the knock at any moment. The kettle cooling in the kitchen made a clicking sound and she thought that was Martin at the door. She knocked her shoe against the side of the coffee table and she thought it was him at the door. Each time her heart rose to bang at the cage of her ribs. What was George saying now?

'. . . anyway Monday or Tuesday.'

'Sorry?'

'Doc says I should be back at work Monday or Tuesday.'

'That's good.'

'You can't come round then?'

'Tuesday?'

'No, tonight.'

'I told you, George. I can't this weekend.'

'I'd have liked a little company.'

'You'll survive.'

'Thank you. Have I done something wrong?'

'No, George. Nothing. I'll explain when I see you. All right? I've got to go.'

She put the phone down, not waiting for his reply and hoping he would not call back. The phone remained silent. She took her case and put it by the door. She washed up the tea things. She unplugged the television. Checked the window locks. Checked her handbag. Money. Keys. Hairbrush. Make-up. Did she need a coat? Just over her shoulders she thought. It wasn't cold.

Martin arrived at eight and refused her offer of a drink. She was glad she had worn the comparatively formal dress as he was wearing a suit. His shirt was white. His shoes, she noticed, highly polished. As she checked the things she had checked ten minutes earlier and he stood by the door she looked at him casually trying to be objective, trying to stand outside herself and everything she had told herself he meant to her. He was attractive, undoubtedly. But it was not the way he looked, it was his presence that made her feel . . . excited, and alive. He exuded a sort of physical power. He made her feel anything could happen. She was sure that was a feeling he did everything to cultivate.

'Are we going far?'

'No.' First rule of discomfiture, offer no supplementary information. In another mood it would be an affectation that would annoy her.

'A hotel?'

'Yes.'

'Is it a surprise?'

'No.'

I don't know where it is so it must be a surprise, she wanted to say but didn't.

He picked up her case without comment on its size and she followed him out into the hall. She stood double-locking the door as he watched.

'You are very beautiful.' The way he said it did not make it sound like a compliment so she did not reply. 'Are you wearing stockings?' He was looking at her ankles.

She followed his gaze, afraid that they had wrinkled. 'Yes.'

He put down the case and folded one arm around her back, pulling her to him and kissing her hard on the mouth. She felt his other hand on the back of the dress moving down to her hem line and pulling the skirt up until his hand rested on the top of the stocking against her cold white flesh. Perhaps he hadn't believed her.

'Would you like to see?'

'Yes.'

He moved back. She held up the skirt of her dress so he could see her thighs. Standing in the hall with her skirts raised; within minutes he had provoked her to that. Her heart was beating faster. She felt hot. In her mind's eye she saw him kneel and kiss the front of her knickers as she stood, skirt in hand, but he did not. She smiled at him.

Outside he opened the car door for her and she got in. He put her case in the boot.

'You make me do extraordinary things.'
'Do I?'
'Why do you suppose that is?'
'A response.'
'To what?'
'To something you want to sense.'
'That isn't there?'
'I didn't say that.'
'Is that what you meant?'
'No. I try to condition your response.'

That was honest. She looked at his profile as he drove. If he had been French he would have had to smoke a Gauloise and wear loose fitting dark grey trenchcoats. Her response to him was extraordinary. It was entirely sexual. She sat there in the passenger seat now not thinking, as she had all week, of whether they were going out of London, what sort of hotel, what sort of restaurants, but of whether she should reach across and take his penis out of his trousers, whether she should take it out and suck it as he drove, or slip her fingers into his shirt and pinch at his nipple and kiss his cheek. Whether she should raise her skirt so he could glimpse her thighs again. She could pay no attention to where they were going. She could think of no pleasant small talk — have you had a busy week, it's awfully nice to get out of the house at the weekend — just how she should respond sexually.

It was a response to him, a psychological and physical response as instinctive as the most primeval response, like a flood of adrenaline at a perceived threat, eyes narrowing, limbs withdrawn, back to something solid. Like a mare in heat, more accurately, mouth sagging, hind legs open, vagina lubricated, nostrils sniffing. It was not a response she could control.

She shifted in her seat, not to get more comfortable but to raise her skirt subtly. With a little surreptitious help from her hand she managed to reveal a suspender and a thin band of white flesh. He did not appear to see but she knew he had.

She put her arm out on to the back of his seat and very gently touched the back of his neck. He looked at her briefly as she did. He put his hand out and touched her knee. He left his hand on her knee.

'Are all men fixated on stockings?' he asked her.

'I don't know.'

'Why not?'

Lack of sophistication was no defence. Was it sophisticated never to have worn stockings in these later years? 'I haven't worn them for a long time.'

'You wear them for me.'

'I do a lot of things for you. I told you. It's part of my response.'

'But I never said anything.'

'I read a lot.'

'About stockings?'

'They're part of the male fantasy.'

'Why didn't you wear them for other men?'

He asked difficult questions. 'To tell you the truth there are a whole lot of reasons.' She thought for a moment. 'Basically because they're so uncomfortable.'

He laughed and she laughed with him, the first time she was aware of a moment of easiness between them. The sexual tension dissipated like water running from a gutter. And immediately she felt she wanted it back. She didn't want ease, comfort, relaxation. She wanted difficulty, stress, excitement. What was happening to her?

It was a big city hotel. An expensive five star hotel The drive had taken thirty minutes. As he drove up at the entrance porters appeared to open both doors. For a second she wondered if he could afford it: that *was* his problem. He gave the porter the keys and took her arm to walk into the hotel. The keys had obviously been accompanied by a large tip, which she had not seen, as the porters bowed and scraped at them both with impressive vigour.

At reception he asked for the room in his own name. Why had she been expecting him to use another? Too many romantic stories about false names and secret rendezvous. Or had she thought he would just be careful. Evidence in a divorce case. He made no attempt to register her. The clerk made no attempt to refer to her. He gave them a credit card. As they waited for the formalities to be completed she saw her case being brought in through the porter's door. It was accompanied by a small black case, like a doctor's bag, and another bigger holdall.

He suggested they have a drink before they went up to the room. The bar in the hotel was plush and elegant. There were semi-circular leather banquettes in the American style around the sides of the room and tables in the middle. All the banquettes appeared to be taken but he found a waiter and in the time it took to pass a generous tip they were shown to a shady corner. She slid along the leather seat and he followed. He ordered a bottle of champagne after he had asked her if she would mind.

Her eyes adjusted to the dim light. At the other side of the bar a pianist picked his way through the popular repertoire of middle-of-the-road classics. A thankless task she thought. And a peculiar art. Playing for no one to hear. Not to play too well or too badly. Just well enough to keep the flow of drinks and conversation lubricated, to cover any silences when small talk runs dry.

He looked at her across the table. She was delighted that the uneasiness had returned. She felt the sexual tension again. Again, she did not think of how good the champagne was or whether she was hungry but whether he would ask her to crawl under the table to him to administer a blow job. The tablecloth would cover a multitude of sinning. And she appeared to have turned into a sinner.

'Is this a regular haunt?' she asked.
'Do I come here often?'
'Well?'
'Only to eat.'
'Not to fuck?'
'No. Until now.' He lifted the champagne glass. 'What shall we drink to?'
'Fantasy.'
'No. Reality.'
'They're the same.' She clinked glasses and sipped at the very dry champagne. It was good. She could feel the nakedness of her thighs above the stocking tops against the back of her dress. She felt wild. Inside, down inside she felt wild, capable of doing anything. Capable of going to the loo, taking off her knickers and have him put his fingers inside her, up inside her, here at the table. Too prosaic. No imagination. No sexual imagination. Capable of developing a wild sexual imagination. Taking her knickers down and pushing them into his mouth so he could taste her on them, smell her on them. There was plenty of time. But she was feeling increasingly impatient. She was having to force herself to sit still. She was tapping her foot enthusiastically to the music. The only release for her energy.

She had wondered before whether he produced this effect on all women, or at least on the women he took out. Now she knew he didn't. It was too special, too specific, too much to do with her and what she wanted and felt at this moment in her life. The theory that the victims of crime were as responsible as the perpetrators again. She had never given it much thought before. Now she knew she had been born to be Martin's victim. She smiled to herself. Or perhaps he had born to be hers.

'Why are you smiling?'

'Private joke.'

'Share it.'

'What's the opposite of victim?'

'Violator.'

'Hadn't thought of that. Well, are you victim or violator?'

'I have no idea. You tell me.'

'That's why I was smiling. I have no idea either.'

'Which would you prefer?'

She thought for a moment. A white silk cord prevented her from closing her legs, closing her cunt.

'I don't know,' she lied.

He poured another glass of champagne from the bottle being careful not to let the water from the ice bucket drip on to her dress. He took her hand and laid it on the table. She left it exactly where he had placed it. He ran his finger up from her knuckle to the web of skin at the top of the finger.

'Remind you of anything?'

She looked down at her hand as he repeated the caress, his finger stroking up from the knuckle then rubbing at the little web of skin. She saw his hand moving from knee to cunt. The little web of skin was incredibly sensitive. Like a cunt. A tiny little cunt.

Three little cunts laying on the table. Open. Her fingers spread. Open. He bent his head and licked at one of the little cunts. The sensation, his wet tongue, his hot breath, was a physical shock. She almost pulled her hand away involuntarily. She almost pulled her hand away deliberately. He smiled at her. It was that infuriating knowing smile. She took her hand away.

'Do you want to eat?'

'No.'

'Let's go to the room then.'

He signed the bill and helped her up from the table. The generously-tipped waiter came hurrying over to deliver over-elaborate goodbyes and thank yous, have-a-nice-evenings and see-you-soons.

They were alone in the lift. He pressed the button for the fourth floor. He kissed her on the cheek. The lift was mirrored. A mirror behind and a mirror above. As he moved back from his kiss she moved to him and kissed him on the mouth. Keeping her eyes open she watched the kiss in the mirror behind. The lift doors slid open. The lift waited patiently.

Martin seemed to know the way to the room. No trying to work out which arrows corresponded with which numbers. 428. Well, it rhymed with fate, wait and late. I can always write a doggerel to immortalise the experience, she thought. He opened the door and let her go in first. Across the threshold.

The room was expensively decorated. A large double bed with a fitted floral counterpane, already turned back to reveal white linen sheets. A television opposite the bed and a drinks fridge tucked away in a corner. Two armchairs and a little table and two upright chairs, with fresh flowers sitting in the middle of the table. The bathroom tiled throughout with shower and bath, brightly lit by fluorescent light in the ceiling. Large white bath towels and white towelling robes. And a view over London from the window.

Neither of them drew the curtains.

'Don't play with me.'

'What have I done?'

'Just don't play games.'

She pulled the dress over her head. She had not put on a slip so now she stood in front of him in black high heels, grey stockings, suspender belt, black french knickers and bra. (More lunchtime expenditure.) She reached behind her and unclipped the bra.

'Come here and fuck me.' She did not say please. She just wanted him inside her with the minimum of ceremony or comment. Her acute desire annoyed her, almost angered her. She didn't care if he took his clothes off or what he did as long as he fucked her now. She turned her back on him and slipped out of her knickers. He had taken his jacket off and his shoes and socks. She came over to him, undid his belt and unzipped his trousers. He pulled them off his legs, hopping from foot to foot.

Stephanie felt wild. She lay on the bed, opened her legs and stroked her pubic hair as she would some small furry animal. It felt independently alive. A pussy? Origin of the expression? Extending her arm further she teased her labia open and patted her clitoris with a finger. He was naked and watching her. She did not care whether he watched or not.

'Don't wait.'

He stood next to the bed, his penis hard, jutting out from his navel. 'What?'

'Just fuck me. Do it.' Her words made her want him more, made her breath faster.

He did exactly as he was told. He lay down beside her then rolled on to her, pushing his weight on to her, crushing her breasts under his chest and coming into her as if by magic. Instant penetration. He was just there. She was so wet and so hot. She took his buttocks in her hands and tried to push him deeper though he was so deep there was no where for him to go but outwards. Outwards and then back in. The hot rod of flesh pierced her again. She caught her breath. She hooked her legs up over his back increasing the penetration. Increasing the pressure on her clitoris. She heard the rasp of her stockings on his flesh. Her mouth was wet, coated in thick saliva like her cunt. Her mouth was hot like her cunt, his tongue hot like his penis and as hard. The perfect match. He was so hard. He plunged into her. Under her hands she could feel the muscles on his buttocks clenched to push. The iron rod seered into her again. Into the jelly of her cunt. She had no control. She could not hold him with her cunt, it was too liquid, she could only feel the hardness of him, his penis, his thighs, his chest, his arms around her neck. And then she came, clinging on to him, levering herself up to him clinging like a drowning man to the branch of a tree, as the chords of feeling joined together in a massive harmony singing in her and around her.

She sank back on to the bed. As if she had had a thirst thoroughly quenched, she felt very little residual desire. She looked at her watch over his shoulder. They had been in the room fifteen minutes. Subtle. He rolled off her, still erect. She encircled his penis with her hand and squeezed. It was incredibly hard. She wanked at it gently, almost absent-mindedly. Her mind, like her eyes, temporarily glazed over.

He got up and went to the bathroom. She heard the shower running. Looking down at herself she realised she had not taken off her shoes. She sat up and swung her legs off the bed. She still felt dissociated from her surroundings. She debated going into the bathroom to wash but decided against it. She found her knickers and put them back on; they immediately clung to her wet cunt. It was not an unpleasant feeling. She straightened the stockings and put her bra back on. Feeling was beginning to return.

He came back into the room. He was completely flaccid. Had it been a cold shower? They both finished dressing. She was hungry now. Ravenously hungry. Now she could allow herself time to eat.

16

It was one of the best meals she had ever had. Delicate, fresh and beautifully presented food; elaborate but cooked in such a way as to bring out the true flavour of the sauce and sauced. Scallops and crab, a round of puff pastry, the lightest butter sauce. Nuggets of lamb stripped of anything but meat grilled and served with carrot puree and crisp haricot beans. A meringue made with hazelnuts, stuffed with raspberries and a rose of fresh cream.

His performance was very different over this meal. Definitely not the egomaniac or, to reserved judgement, the egomaniac making a hearty attempt to find someone else at least as fascinating as himself. He asked questions. Listened to the answers. Asked supplementary questions as a result of the answers — to prove he'd listened? From the cradle to the grave, well, at least to her present employment. Parents, place of birth, star sign (a mistake perhaps, he seemed to know nothing about star signs), schooling, university, first job.

A virtuoso performance, she thought. It was not until the dessert that her hunger was truly satisfied. It was not until the coffee that she found that the story of her life was more or less complete (a sad commentary, life measured if not in a coffeespoon then only three courses and a half a cup of coffee) and she could ask a question of him.

'Why didn't you want to come?' She was obsessed with sex.

He smiled more broadly than she had ever seen him. A smile that transformed his face, made it older, avuncular, slightly unpleasant. 'I was hungry.'

'Not for me?'

'It's not necessary.'

'What?'

'My pleasure doesn't have to be orgasmic. That's such an old sexual cliché. I can have pleasure without.'

'And were you hungry?'

'Do you think the sole aim of sex is orgasm?'

She thought about it. It had never occurred to her to think about it before. 'Yes.'

'I don't.'

'Especially when you're hungry,' he smiled. He laid his hand on top of hers. 'We're very good in bed.'

'Yes.'

'You said I make you feel something. It's the same for me, what you make me feel.'

'You're more in control.'

'Only of the situation.'

She wanted to go on, ask him if that was really true, ask him if he had ever experienced sex as good before, ask him if he'd done to another woman what he'd done to her. But she stopped herself. Not because she thought it would matter to him but because actually she didn't want to know nor did she want to talk about it any more. What happened in bed between them happened. It was its own explanation, for the moment at least. More coffee please, but not another brandy.

They talked about other things. He touched her as they talked, laying his hand on her shoulder, her arm, her hand. His hands felt cold. It made her want to shiver but she managed not to. Earlier, over the food, she had forgotten the effect his physical presence had on her, but now as one need was satiated another arose, and the feeling was there again; a breathlessness, the inability to think about anything other than his nearness. It was like feeling a drug beginning to work; like taking an aspirin for a headache feeling the blood carrying the drug up to the brain, feeling the ache dissolve and wash away. Except that this drug washed away no aches; it created them, enlarged them, placed them in positions where they pushed aside other things, other concerns, other priorities, until it sat massive and alone. The ache for Martin.

She would have liked to say that she wanted to go up to the bedroom but she felt she had been so demanding before dinner that to repeat the performance now might be avaricious. She accepted another cup of coffee from the offering waiter.

'You don't seem to care that I'm married.'

That was completely out of the blue. She had not wanted his wife to sit at the table with them. 'I don't.'

'Why not?'

'Does it matter?'

'No. Just curious.'

'If you weren't married I don't think I'd have ever seen you again after that night at my flat.'

'It makes you feel safe.'

'Exactly.'

If he was satisfied with such a glib response she saw no reason why she shouldn't be. It might even be the truth.

In the lift she felt her heart beat increase. They were not alone so he made no attempt to kiss her but his still cold hand reached out for hers. He did not lace his fingers into hers but instead made a circle by touching his middle finger to his thumb and holding two of her fingers there. The ring and the stone. She looked at him and he stared back into her eyes. Joke.

Outside the bedroom door, as he found the key and fitted it into the lock, she realised that her mouth was slightly dry; some psychological reaction to her increased heart rate, she supposed. She swallowed hard. The body's reaction to excitement was so prosaic. In fact, of course, it was anticipation of excitement. Behind the green baize door. Behind closed doors. Her secret. He opened the door and stood aside for her to go in. As far as she could judge his face was expressionless.

Stephanie sat on the corner of the bed, her hands in her lap. He said nothing. Picking up the small black case he put it on the table but did not open it. He sat down on the bed beside her and unzipped her dress. She made no attempt to help him as he pulled it down from her arms until it lay around her waist. He stood, taking her by the arm to make her stand too. The dress would not fall to the floor; it had to be pulled over her head. He gathered it in his hands and stretched it up over her head. He held her just above both elbows and with downward pressure indicated that she should sit again. She felt unable to move.

He hung the dress up neatly and went into the bathroom. She sat unmoving, her hands in her lap.

Her hands felt light, numb, unmuscled. She knew she was giving a performance but it was not a performance for his sake. She was doing it for herself and for what it made her feel, and for that reason she wanted the performance to be perfect. She heard him undress but did not turn her head towards the bathroom when he came out. She waited until he came into the line of vision she had from where she sat on the bed.

He was wearing a towel knotted around his waist. From the outline of the towel she could see that he was not yet erect. He stood in front of her, flicking her hair out from the back of her neck until he could touch the bare flesh. He rested his cold hand there. By the slightest pressure he made her look up at his face. He did not smile.

'Take your bra off.'

She obeyed, quickly replacing her hands in her lap the task was completed. She felt the sides of her breasts pressed against the flesh of her upper arms. Her breasts felt heavy, the nipples light.

He licked a finger and immediately transferred the saliva to her left nipple. The sudden contact made her catch her breath. The tip of his finger made little circles on her hardened nipple but the touch was not hard, not even firm. It was the lightest touch, the softest touch like being brushed with the petal of a rose. He licked his finger again and wet the other nipple, again using the lubricant to ease the circling movements he made with his fingertip.

He held both nipples between thumb and forefinger and simultaneously pinched both; not hard but not gently either. He ran his hand down the valley between her breasts pushing them outward against her upper arms. He ran his hand under each breast finding the crease that they made under their own weight. He lifted them as though weighing them in his hands. And all this time he stood in front of her looking down at her, looking down at his hands working on her breasts. And all this time she sat with hands in her lap, not looking at his face.

He moved behind her. She heard the black case being opened but did not look to see what he was taking from it. She wanted to know, she wanted to see; she wanted to know everything that was in the case but she knew that was against the rules. Her rules. His rules. The rules. She remained passive, feeling the remnants of sensation his hands had left in her breasts.

Martin sat behind her on the bed. She could feel the side of his towel against her naked back. He kissed her between her shoulder blades and up to the nape of her neck, holding her hair out of the way with his hands. Then he knelt on the bed behind her and reached around with both hands to cup her breasts and pull her back towards him. Now she could feel his erection stabbing out from the towel into the small of her back just above the clasp of her suspender belt. He kissed her back again.

She felt him move back slightly. No contact now, not even his penis in her back. He smoothed her hair down with his hand where he had lifted it to kiss her neck and then pulled a black velvet blindfold over her head. It was sculptured at the front to nose and cheeks and fitted perfectly. She sat open-eyed and could see nothing. After a moment, as her eyes adjusted, the faintest light seeped in through the edges of the material but not enough to allow any sort of vision.

'Have you done this before?'
'Who have you done this with?'
'How long have you been doing this?'
'Does this excite you?'
'Does this excite you more than anything?'
'What if I did it to you?'
'Who taught you?'

'Who did you do this to first? Who was she? What was she to you?'

'Shall I spoil the game and move?'

'Where did you get this blindfold? Did your wife make it? Does she make all your equipment? Do you do this with your wife? Do you do this with every woman? Why are you making me do this? Or am I making you do this? Am I making you do this? Is this your response to me or my response to you? I never told you how much this excites me? Did I? Did I?'

'What are you going to do next?'

Stephanie wanted to ask all these questions but remained silent. She sat, hands in her lap, knees together, the black velvet covering her eyes.

Now there was no temptation to look round to see what he was doing. She felt him get off the bed. She discovered she could not hear footsteps on the carpeted floors; perhaps he wasn't moving. Then she felt his hands on her arms pulling her into a standing position. She stood and he moved her away from the bed slightly so she did not have the comfort of feeling the bed against the back of her knees. She supposed he was kneeling now because his hands were moving up one of her legs, one at the back, one at the front, from ankle to upper thigh, caressing the stocking, smoothing it, gliding over the suspender up over the white exposed flesh, just brushing the lace of the french knickers, then down again. Very slowly. Very lightly. The same with the other leg. Then higher, both hands moving over her buttocks up to her waist. The same soft gentle movement. Over her navel, over her hips. Up to the waist again.

His hands took hold of the knickers at the waist and pulled them down to her ankles. Not gently as he had done before, but suddenly, as if he was losing patience.

He guided her feet out of them by holding her ankle, indicating with an upward pressure that she should raise her foot. The same with the other ankle. He flipped the knickers clear then pulled her ankle over to one side so she stood with her legs apart, the perfect marionette, her legs opened enough to expose her labia and her pubic hair still matted together from the frantic sex of earlier.

'Put your hands together in front of you.'

The perfect performance. She obeyed immediately. A soft material fell across her wrists. In a moment her hands were bound together. She could not resist the temptation to test the efficacy of his work and she wriggled her wrists against the bonds. The scout had tied his knots. There was no escape. And she had to admit to herself she was glad she had tried to get free because the knowledge that she couldn't, that the bonds were not a thin charade, thrilled her instantly.

'Lie down in the middle of the bed.'

She wasn't sure she knew where the bed was any more but she inched back until she felt it against the back of her knees and sat down. It was difficult to sit down with your hands tied: no balancing controls. She edged to her left but felt the edge of the bed so moved to the right until she was far enough over to be more or less in the middle of what she imagined was the foot of the bed. Then she lay back, difficult again, and putting her feet up used her legs to lever herself back until she felt the pillow.

'Good.'

The awkwardness of movement excited her: the foreignness of not being able to reach out with a hand. Her breath was coming in short pants. My God. He seemed to know exactly what to make her do to get her feeling . . . Just feeling. Feeling everything. Feeling sexually awake. Feeling everything, every part of her alive, every part of her sexually alive. What he had just made her do, crawling across the bed on her back, made her feel her thighs, her knees, her elbows. Made her feel exposed. Open. Made her feel wanton and wild. It had occurred to her, the first time he had tied her in his house, that he was trading in on the male belief that all women have a fantasy about being raped. It was true in part of course, provided, and provided very strictly, that the rapist was incredible attractive, that the scene of the crime was exotic and glamorous, that actually the rape itself had as much violence, as much real violence, as an over-enthusiastic embrace, and that the difference between saying 'stop' and meaning 'stop' were always clearly understood. But what she felt now, what he was doing now, was quite different. Not the stuff of clichéd fantasy.

He was pulling her hands above her head. He tied them to the headboard. She immediately tried to pull them down again without success. She felt his hands on her ankle. Felt him tie it presumably to the leg of the bed. And then the other ankle, spreading her legs open as he had done before, spreading her open across the bed as he tied the other leg. She tried to pull her legs away. The bonds were firm. Tight and firm. Just as before. Open and spread as before. His. The wave of pleasure rolled over her then ebbed away, sucking her down with the sand and the pebbles.

He was not on the bed. She imagined he was standing at the foot of the bed, immediately in front of her open cunt looking at it, looking at her. Staring at her. She hoped so. She could not hear him move. She could not hear a sound other than her own breathing, her own excited breathing. She wanted him to do a thousand things to her. Pinch her nipples. Rub her breasts.

Stroke her clitoris. Kiss her clitoris. Suck her. Suck her nipples. Bite her nipples. Fill her with his fingers, with his penis. Lie on her. His full weight on her. His full penis in her. Pull her up off the bed against the bonds, pull her out of her bonds. Kiss her mouth. Tongue her mouth. Kiss her thighs. Tease her. Tease. Touch and tease. Touch her arms, her inner arms, her lips, her navel, her knees. She writhed against her bonds trying to move towards him, to push her cunt up at him wherever he was, make herself more open, more desirable. To provoke him. He did nothing. She stopped moving and listened turning her head from side to side to catch any sound.

She heard him pick up the telephone. She heard him dial. Seven numbers. Waiting. She could not hear a ringing tone.

'Hello. She's ready. As I promised.'

She heard him kneel between her open legs. The bed gave under his weight. He leant forward and licked her cunt, long wet licks like a child exaggeratedly licking an ice lolly, the tip of his tongue starting at the opening of her vagina and licking up to her clitoris. Long wet licks, covering her already wet labia with his own saliva. His hands held her on either side of her hips, steadying himself. Long wet licks. At the clitoris his tongue seemed to pause, flicking at the little bud, intensifying the sensation.

She moaned quietly. She could not help herself. It was not a cumulative pleasure, like the pleasure that would bring her to orgasm, but each stroke was its own pleasure, a little monument of pleasure complete in itself.

Martin stopped. His hands moved from her hips to her breasts. He began to knead at her breasts, squeeze and knead them. Taking great handfuls of flesh in each hand he pulled them upwards, sideways, down towards her navel, made circles of her flesh, made intricate patterns, figures of eight, Greek letters. Kneading and squeezing. Stopping to release them momentarily while he took one nipple or both nipples, pinched them, pulled them out from her breast, pushed them down into her breast, tweaked them lightly or strongly.

He got up from the bed. He had built a fire in her breasts, a lake in her cunt. She lay, unable to move, unable to do anything but feel the pleasure he was giving her. She was glad he had stopped. Or rather she was glad he had stopped playing with her; without his coming inside her she could not take much more.

The silence was broken by a knock at the door. The phone call. She had forgotten the phone call. She knew, of course, that he hadn't made a call. It was part of the game. What was extraordinary to her was that he knew this had been her fantasy. He knew she had fantasised a stranger last time he had tied her to his bed, fantasised a grizzled hoary stranger thrusting into her. How had he known, how could he have known? And now he was performing for her.

It was a performance. Perhaps she said that to herself a little too emphatically. It was a performance. The knock on the door again. It was him knocking on the door from the inside. It was him. It *was*. She heard him open the door. She listened intently trying to keep her body perfectly still, trying to keep her breathing under control so she could hear less of herself and more of what went on in the room. She was certain she could only hear him breathing.

'Don't make a sound.' She heard him walk over to the bed. She couldn't hear another set of footsteps but she could barely hear footsteps at all. Almost instinctively she tried to close her legs, pull her thighs together. The bonds allowed a little movement, but too little to make any difference. And it didn't make any difference because there was no stranger.

'As I promised, you see. Just as I promised.'

There was silence. She listened. No movement. Then a hand, the back of a hand against her cheek. She realised she had almost stopped breathing. She tried to relax.

He sprung on her like a tiger. Leapt on her, his full weight landing on her body, his penis pounding into her navel and then in a second embedded deep in her cunt, so suddenly she had no sensation of thrusting, just the immediate hardness of him deep inside her. Hardness like iron. Coldness like iron. He felt cold in her. He was pumping in and out of her now, breathing heavily. It was him. She had never heard him breathe like this before. It was him. The stranger tore at her, gripping her breasts, slipping his hands under her buttocks to pull her up to him as he thrust, pushing a hand down between their bodies so his finger could rub at her clitoris, rub at it, prod it, pull it. Breathing faster and faster. It was Martin. She told herself it was Martin. Then she told herself it was not. It was the stranger. The gnarled stranger, the knotted craggy cock, the blue veins, the black hair, the ugly knotted cock; foul breath, dirty stranger, inside her delicate flower of a cunt. Inside her. Taking her. His enormous cock filling her. His sperm ready to spout into her. His dirty sperm, his stained yellowing sperm, in her.

She had no control of her orgasm. It was not in her cunt but in her mind. Her mind was sending the pleasure down to her cunt, her breasts, the clitoris he was pushing at. It was only a matter of seconds before the orgasm in her mind was overtaken, bettered, covered by the orgasm in her cunt. She thought she heard a scream, her scream. Forgetting the bonds she tried to bring her arms around him. The sudden jerk from wrists and ankles, she was bound, unable to move, that feeling pushed her down into her orgasm even deeper down into the dark of it, the darkness in her eyes, the moving throbbing darkness in her mind. And then she felt his penis swelling and throbbing, felt his back arch out and his penis withdraw to plunge into her for the last time, felt its plunge and then his hot shooting sperm. And that took her deeper still. Like three orgasms, three seamless orgasms, so much part of each other, that each made the other deeper, bigger, more full of raw endless sensation that she knew would have to end.

He lay on her breathing more evenly. She could feel his penis begin to shrink inside her. She could feel his sperm begin to trickle down her cunt. Not for a moment did it occur to her that is was a stranger lying on top of her. The fantasy was over. *That* fantasy.

It was strange not being able to hug him. She wanted to wrap her arms around him. The fact that she couldn't still, to her surprise, provided the faintest thrill, a *frisson* of realisation that her position was still vulnerable and exposed. She was still open. Still wild. She stopped herself. Better not pursue that thought. Too much excitement. It'll end in tears as her mother would say. And she banished that line of thought quickly too, her mother didn't belong in this bedroom, near this bed.

17

Martin untied her ankles and then her wrists. He massaged them as he did so but there was very little discomfort.

'Close your eyes against the light.' He rolled the blindfold off her eyes. It took a moment before she could see properly again. She realised he had not kissed her on the mouth while she had been tied to the bed and she wanted to be kissed now. She sat up on the bed.

'Kiss me.'

He took her in his arms and kissed her on the mouth his tongue vying with hers for territory. She hugged him to her, relishing the sensation that a few minutes earlier had been denied. It felt good to be able to hug him, pull him into her, squeeze him. His mouth felt good too. Warm, welcoming. Normal. Comfortingly normal. (Reassurance after depravity? Is that what she thought it had been — depravity?)

There was a moment when the kiss could have ended, when they could have broken free from each other's arms and sat on the bed to talk, perhaps, to have a drink and be polite. But that moment had passed, was passing. Far from feeling sated and sexually exhausted she found the kiss was making her heart beat faster again, pulling her mind back to thoughts of sexual excitement, making her hands caress him more specifically, more urgently, more rhythmically.

They lay back on the bed. Stephanie couldn't tell whether he'd pulled her over or she'd pushed him, but they ended with her on top. She started to kiss his neck, his chest moving her hands over his chest as though to blaze the trial for her mouth. He was still flaccid. She could feel his slack wet cold penis just below her breasts as she moved down his body. She took him in her hand and squeezed gently. Then she slid further down the bed and took him in her mouth. He tasted different. He tasted of her, of course, her saltiness, her juices. It did not bother her. She circled the tip of his penis with her tongue, nudging it, sucking it gently, then more strongly. She wanted to feel him stir, feel the blood begin to pump back into him, feel him grow inside her mouth until he filled it and she could sit on him, push her cunt down on him, have him in her again and again and again.

It was a little while before she realised her efforts were having no effect. He was not swelling in her mouth, he was not growing. Instinctively — she had no reason for thinking it would excite him — she pivoted round until her thighs were level with his head, so he could see her pubic hair opposite his head. He took the hint and pulled her up over him, adjusting himself until his head lay down under her cunt as her mouth continued to suck at his penis. Looping his arms around her waist for leverage he pulled himself up to the lips of her cunt and started to kiss her. Her instinct had been right. She had felt the effect that just moving into this position had had on his penis; now what he was doing to her increased his own excitement. His penis began to uncurl. She pulled her mouth away for a moment to watch as the flaccid flesh began to blossom like some strange tropical fruit. Then she covered him with her mouth again using her tongue to coat him with saliva and tease and stroke his now almost full length. Trying, for a moment, to ignore what he was doing to her, and concentrate on him.

Straight sex. What she'd done before a million times. Well many times. Good clean fun. It was good, it felt good and perhaps if this had happened earlier and nothing else was going to happen other than straight intercourse it would never have occurred to her that this was less than exciting. But that was not the case now. He had changed her perspective. The light came from a different direction; different shadows and different highlights. Other things had happened. And she wanted them to continue to happen. She was not here to have a George, or even a Devlin.

Martin may have felt her enthusiasm wane, her concentration lapse. He may have felt that she was not applying herself to the job in hand with much verve. He may have sensed that she was not responding to the contact of his mouth on her cunt. His sexual sensitivity to her was acute, she knew that. And obviously it was a mutual sensitivity, because she was aware of a change in mood in him before he started to move.

This time she was sure who it was applying the pressure. He was. He was pushing her over and getting out from under her. His penis popped out of her mouth. It glistened with her saliva. It looked angry. One angry eye. She sensed he was angry and knew she was innocent. That was the performance. Her renowned innocence.

He was pushing her again moving her on to her stomach. In her mind she wanted to make a round 'O' of her mouth and ask him what he was doing. He got up off the bed but almost before she could look round he was back again. He kissed her between the shoulder blades, a hard kiss pushing his head down on to her so she was pressed into the bed covers. He moved his mouth so he could kiss the nape of her neck, clearing her hair away with his hand. He was kneeling now, knees either side of her thighs, and she could feel his hard penis resting against her buttocks.

She opened her legs so he could kneel between them, then raised her buttocks so his penis slipped down between her legs. In this position her breasts hung down from her chest and his hands immediately reached round her to clasp and fondle them. He pinched her nipples hard then pulled them down until they were almost touching the bedclothes. His penis was between the lips of her cunt but it would need a hand to press it into the right position for penetration. As it was, he was rocking it back and forward along the narrow wet slit, nudging her clitoris at teach movement.

Stephanie felt him reach out and a moment later was aware of a cold wet sensation around the puckered hole of her arse. My god he was going to bugger her. Bugger her! His fingers were working the lubricant around the hole and up into it. His finger was inside her arse. Then she felt him greasing his penis.

She had never been buggered and couldn't even remember an attempt. Now she appeared to be seconds away from it. Unless she acted now, unless she pulled herself up off the bed or did something. Of course she had no intention of doing anything, anything other than feeling the extraordinary sensations that were racing through her. Her most immediate reaction had been panic and shock. Now those feelings were mixed, interlaced with total excitement. It was like being a virgin again. She couldn't help feeling a sense of fear too; everyone had said it would be painful. But God it was exciting. He was exciting.

He leant forward again and was gently pushing his penis up against her hole. She could feel its heat and hardness so clearly, more clearly than with her cunt because there were no hot wet fleshy lips to confuse the sensation. Then he pushed into her. She felt her arse give, felt it try to accommodate his width and fail. She was too tense. The muscles were contracted and hard. She must relax. (Why must she? Why didn't she tell him to go to hell?) She made a effort to relax the muscles and he responded immediately pushing his penis home. It was in. She couldn't tell how far. The whole thing was so different, the feelings, the wetness, the heat, the geometry of their bodies. A whole world of newness. But he was inside her arse. She felt him push again and this time she could feel, or thought she could feel, him move deeper. He was still not fully home. She could tell because she couldn't feel his navel against her buttocks or his balls down between her labia.

For that moment the concentration had swamped her excitement. Now as he began to move inside her, move back and forth as though fucking her, and each stroke upward taking him deeper and nearer to being all the way home, she could feel her excitement reassert itself. It hurt, but it was not painful. Or it might have been painful but for the other things converting the pain into pleasure. She was moaning. She could hear herself moaning. She was breathing in short gasps. There was something so different about having this sword of flesh inside her here, in her arse, and that alone was swelling all her sexual awareness.

Her mind told her what was being done to her. The

words repeated in her mind over and over again. 'I'm being buggered.' 'He's buggering me.' 'Buggering me.' The words were an incitement to her other senses.

It was so like intercourse. The rhythm. The feeling of a penis buried deep inside her body. And yet her cunt was free. Her clitoris untouched. Her vagina empty. Penetrated and full of his penis; a penis deep inside her and yet her cunt unused. That was the strangest sensation.

He was all the way home now. On his upward strokes she could feel his balls bounce into her labia and his navel push into her buttocks. She seemed to be so wet down there. She wasn't sure where all the lubrication was coming from but now he had no trouble moving freely in and out of her. He was breathing heavily and started to moan. He was near orgasm. She was nowhere near.

He moaned in rhythm to his action. His hands held her hips to pull her back on to him until he stopped and leant forward on to her arched back. His hand went under her and found her clitoris. It was actually cold. He pushed at it hard. He rubbed at it in a way which could only be described as vicious. He was angry again. Angry that she was not excited. He had to make her excited. He was rough. He plunged his fingers into her cunt. Suddenly she could feel herself penetrated in two places, could feel his fingers up alongside his penis inside her, separated only by some thin membrane of her own.

Then he was up again and holding her hips to steady himself as he ploughed into her with complete abandon. He was not being careful, he was not making sure he hurt her as little as possible, he was only concerned with himself, with coming hard and hot in her arse, right up in her arse where he wanted to be.

And she was concerned with the very same thing. She pushed her buttocks out at him, ignoring any pain, relishing the pain, turning the pain to intense pleasure, wanting him there, wanting to know she'd been buggered by him. She pushed her buttocks back into his navel, feeling his balls, feeling her breasts bouncing under the effort, her nipples grazing the bedclothes. She listened as his rhythmic moans became one long moan and realised that she was moaning too for exactly the same reason. Somehow this man was bringing her off; his action, motion, was making her shake into orgasm. He came first but as she felt him relax slightly and pull back she came too, an orgasm like none she had ever had, an orgasm seated in her clitoris and caused by lack of touch, caused by absence in the presence of total excitement. An orgasm of the head pulsing through her body. An orgasm so unlike anything she had felt before she wondered whether it was an orgasm at all.

A delicious feeling of relaxation overtook her suddenly. She curled up slightly and decided she would just close her eyes and rest, just for a moment. He lay beside her unmoving. In the darkness behind her closed eyes she felt a rush toward sleep, felt consciousness pulling away from her like a boat accelerating away and leaving the shore far behind, so that in a matter of minutes it was impossible to see the barest suggestion of land.

From somewhere in sleep some part of her registered that he had turned off the light. It did nothing to deter her from sleep.

18

The light woke her. They hadn't drawn the curtains of the room and light was flooding in. It may have been the noise too; the hotel was alive with the sound of trolleys wheeled down corridors, plumbing in adjacent rooms as occupants peed and washed, the obsequious knocks of room-service waiters. It might have been the cold. Since the room had felt so hot last night, and since she had only meant to sleep fleetingly, she had not got into bed. Now she was cold.

He was lying next to her, wide awake, but wearing the hotels towelling robe. For a second she had to admit to disappointment. In her fantasy, he would not have been here. He would have gone. Gone to return again by all means, but not lying next to her in the morning to present immediate problems; problems like whether she should kiss him. Her mouth felt awful, dry and acid and she didn't particularly want him pushing his tongue into such unsavouriness. Problems like what on earth she looked like to him. She had slept with all her make-up on. The exertions of the night would probably have made inroads in her carefully prepared hair. She was sure she looked like the inside of her mouth felt.

The tradition was to dive for the bathroom and lock the door to emerge in half-an-hour radiant and fully restored. That was a possibility of course, but it was not one she really wanted to take.

'Feel all right?'

'Thirsty,' she replied.

'Coffee? Tea?'

'Coffee.'

He picked up the phone. He ordered coffee not asking her if she wanted to eat anything. She didn't.

'It's got colder. It was so hot in here last night.'

'Hotel central heating. Everyone takes baths in the morning so it gets colder. By eleven it'll be boiling again.'

'It's not really cold out.'

'Hotels like to keep the rooms hot. Encourages drinking.'

She got up and found the other towelling robe. The mirror by the wardrobe confirmed her worst fears; she combed her hair with her fingers but with little effect. She sat on the edge of the bed.

'No more illusions.'

'About what?'

'The carefully prepared image of modern woman.'

'Is that what it was.'

'What a woman's best friend always tells her. Never go to bed in your make-up.'

'To go to bed to sleep you mean.'

'Yes.'

'You're supposed to perform as a harlot then, when the performance is over, trot into the bathroom and come out looking like the cover girl from *Health and Beauty*.'

'Absolutely. And this is why.'

He stared into her face as though looking for

evidence. 'I find you very attractive. But then every man you've ever known has said that to you, haven't they?'

'No.'

'Tell the truth. In some form or another that's what they've said.'

'Yes, I suppose so. I don't feel very attractive now.'

'Stand up.' There was sudden authority in his voice as if there were roles to be played again. Small talk over. Surely he didn't want that game at this time in the morning. But she couldn't break the pattern, nor did she really want to. She stood.

'Take your robe off.' She let the robe fall to the floor. Clearly the game was on.

'I've never seen you naked in the light before. Not in natural light.' He did nothing but look at her. She stood stock-still but this time she watched him as his eyes roamed around her body. She saw him staring at her breasts, saw his eyes flick from one to the other, then down to her pubis.

'Put one leg up on that chair.'

This brought her labia into view from where he sat on the bed. He would not be able to see much, she was sure, because the pubic hair needed to be parted after being matted down during the night. That was what he had in mind. But he hesitated. It was not like him to be coy.

'It's your turn.'

'What is?'

'Now.'

'I don't want a turn.' Turn and turn again.

'Then I want to see your cunt.'

She reached down between her thighs and felt among her tight pubic curls to find her opening. Pulling a finger along the slit she pushed the hairs aside until her finger spread her nether lips to his gaze. Wrinkled, long gills from red to pink to dark brown. It took two or three attempts before the hairs curled out of the way and she would feel she was exposed. She could also feel, by this time, a glimmer of sexual arousal. Except the coffee was coming. She wanted to go on stroking herself for him, in front of him, but the coffee was coming.

'Touch your clitoris.'

'The coffee . . .'

'Do as I say.'

'The waiter'll come in.'

'Do as I say.'

Stephanie put the tip of her finger against her clitoris and deliberately tapped it fast and hard. It was the one movement of her hand she had discovered over the years made her more excited than any other. Suddenly she wanted to get turned on and get turned on fast. She didn't give a damn about the waiter. Let him come in and have a good look too. She moved her hand down to stroke the whole of her cunt even dipping her finger inwards when she reached the opening to her vagina. She was wet. Not soaking like last night, but wet enough to slide in and out easily, wet enough to allow her finger to glide quickly up to her clitoris again to tap out the familiar message.

He watched her finger move. She watched his face, watched his eyes. She saw his erection grow under the robe. He looked up and stared into her eyes. There was a knock at the door and a rattle of keys.

'Don't move. Don't stop. Don't.'

A moment of panic seized her, the bravado gone. Standing naked in broad daylight, one foot on a chair, her hand working between her legs. Perhaps a sight the waiter had seen many times. But he had never seen her. Then she realised that the little corridor into the room would prevent the waiter seeing anything assuming he was met at the door. And he had gone to the door.

He looked back at her reprovingly. She began her work again easing her hand down to her vagina. He opened the door. She could not see the waiter so obviously he could not see her.

'Morning sir.'

'Morning.'

'Your coffee. Shall I put it on the table sir?' Stephanie was standing by the table.

'No, I'll take it.' A feeling of infinite relief. As if to thank him she tapped at her clitoris again though she felt no sensation from it.

'Right then sir.'

'Hold on a minute . . .' What was he doing now? My God, what was he doing?

'. . . I think we've got some dirty things from last night.' There was nothing and he knew it. She looked towards the door. From the little corridor he appeared, then just as the waiter would have come into sight he stopped. 'No sorry. My mistake.'

She heard the door close. He put the tray down on the bed and sat in a chair opposite her.

'Now do it.' And she wanted to. She wanted to make herself come. She wanted to come in front of him, spray out in front of him, show him how she could bring herself off, show him his little game had not scared her, had not put her off, had not made her feel any less sexy than she had before.

She worked more slowly at first. Long slow strokes. She let her other hand pinch at each of her nipples in turn, then squeeze them, knead them, push them into her chest and round in circles like lumps of unleavened dough. She wanted to put on a show for him and for his waiter friend. Bring the waiter back on. Bring all the waiters back on. She could show them something they've never seen.

She moved to lay on the bed stretching across it then took up the rhythm again. The little dip into her vagina, the long stroke from there to her clitoris, the tapping on her clitoris then back down to her vagina again. She arched her back off the bed, spreading her legs as wide as she could, then left her breasts and pulled one of her legs back towards her chest so the split of her cunt was totally open and exposed to him. She pulled her leg back against her chest, as far back as she could, hooking her elbow around her knee. This stretched her labia, pulling out the sensitive tissue.

She looked around and saw Martin standing now in front of her cunt looking up into it. She wished there were other men too, all with bulges in their trousers where their cocks pleaded for freedom. All the hotel waiters. He had loosened the robe so his cock was free and he circled it with his fist, wanking it towards her.

She was moving faster now, her hand not dipping into her vagina as it interrupted the rhythm too much. She wanted fast long strokes and urgent hard tapping on her clitoris. She pulled back on her leg again feeling her breast and the top of her thigh pressed together, feeling the tight hard nipple in the middle of all that white flesh.

She wanted other men there, wanted their greedy eyes staring at her. Wanted to see them take out their cocks, cocks made hard by her display. Wanted to see them wank on her, for her, over her. Wanted to watch Martin as they did. All the waiters in their white linen coats. They had never seen a woman like this, like her. Not in all their years in hotel bedrooms, all those years of copulation and nakedness surprised, had they ever seen this.

She could feel her excitement. There was no need to go fast any more. There was no need to stroke any more, just the tapping on the nut of her clitoris, the smallest of movements, the tiniest of rhythms would bring her off now, as she held her eyes open and watched the eye of his penis emerge then disappear again as he moved his hand up and down on it. She came sharply, quickly and intensely.

The coffee was cold.

He was sensitive in other ways. He went out to get newspapers. She was sure that was just an excuse, just a way of letting them both have a little privacy, but she appreciated it. She had wanted to be alone and wouldn't have known how to ask.

So she lay in the bath grateful for the time to think. He had discovered her nipples and cunt were sore, obviously as a result of the night's activities. The wages of sin. The sins of the flesh. (What would my mother say?) Her reaction to him was, she thought, what it must be like to be a nymphomaniac. The constant and total desire for sex, a desire never satisfied but only temporarily assuaged, an assuagement lasting for shorter and shorter periods of time.

Of course, with her it was not the desire for sex. It was the desire for sex with Martin. And it wasn't just sex. What he was doing to her was not sex in any sense she had understood it before. It was a total involvement of all her senses but most of all of her mind; it was her mind that he had released. It was her mind that was producing the extraordinary sensations she was experiencing, because her mind had taken flight. He had released her fantasies; made her see how to use them. Actually, to be accurate, he had first made her create fantasies, embroidered, elaborate fantasies and then shown her how to use them. She had never thought of herself as inhibited, sexually or in any other way, but he had freed her of any inhibition and allowed her to go wild. Wild.

She could not help but smile to herself at the thought of things she had done last night and this morning and the absolute pleasure she had experienced. She certainly had no regrets. No regrets about what she had done, and no regrets about her fantasies, the fantasies that she knew had carried her away on a wave of passion.

The idea of nymphomania she knew had occurred to her for one reason. Even lying in the bath now she knew she wanted more, she wanted it to happen again. And again. And again? That was the question, wasn't it? Where would it end? Would sensation-seeking inevitably end unhappily? (A moral tale.) Would she want to take it further? As she had fantasised being bound and made this come true — however complex the procedure she was absolutely certain she had made him make it come true — would she want her other fantasies produced like rabbits from a hat as the milder thrills began to wear of? Would she want to see the waiters leering down at her, want them to wank over her?

What had happened to her fantasy of tying him down, dominating him? It had been strong at the beginning of the relationship. Overpoweringly strong. Now it had disappeared completely, replaced by its absolute and exact opposite. He had tossed the coin from heads to tails, obverse to reverse. Would she ever want to toss it back again?

The water suddenly struck her as cold and she got out of the bath and rubbed herself dry. He was right about the heating. It was after eleven now and the room was boiling again.

She went into the bedroom, took out her make-up bag, and sat in front of the mirror. Her face, bright pink from being scrubbed clean, stared back at her earnestly. For some reason she half-expected it to be changed.

Stephanie had gone further last night than she had at his house. She knew she had gone further in her mind as well as physically and she knew she wanted to go further again. Her physical satisfaction had been enormous but it was a satisfaction that needed renewal not one that was complete in itself. So that was undoubtedly her major problem. She had never been addicted, even to cigarettes, but as she thought of not continuing, perhaps not seeing him again, the feeling she got, the feeling of total need, was she thought, like the feeling of needing a cigarette when you smoked eighty a day.

She told herself she was being silly. She was in control. She had known exactly what she was doing in agreeing to this weekend, she had known exactly why she was doing it. She knew she wanted to repeat the experience she had had at his house. It was as simple as that. She had repeated the experience, successfully given the performance and would do it again later. After that, perhaps it would be an end in itself. Perhaps she would not want to see him again. There was still no friendship between them certainly no love. A mutual interest held them together; the mutual interest happened to be sex.

That sounded convincing at least. That is what she could believe. And it was something like the truth. Something. After all she remembered what Joyce had said. Her fantasy sex had ended like turning out a light.

That's clearly what would happen. The fantasy sex syndrome. A new psychological insight. A new insight into the workings of the human mind. More likely a very old insight, a very old syndrome; what was new was that it was no longer a man's prerogative. Now women were free to worry about obsessive sexual behaviour. Liberated to enjoy a new set of neuroses.

No, she thought, that was probably not the case at all. The male fantasy sex syndrome was in all probability entirely different. She must ask Martin. So far she had carefully avoided all the questions she really wanted to ask him. Or rather, she had asked partial questions and he had given her partial replies. Fair enough, since they were sharing a partial relationship, an uneasy partial friendship in a partial affair. Only the sex was whole.

If she asked him a whole question, a straightforward no-nonsense question, there was every chance she might get a straightforward, no-nonsense answer. How long have you been tying women to beds? And a straightforward supplementary question. What percentage of women like it a) immensely, b) somewhat, c) a little, d) not at all? Answer: Ten years. a) 61%, b) 12%, c) 6%, d) 2% and the rest didn't know.

What she had to work out for herself was whether she actually wanted to hear the answers. It seemed to her that such candour might put the relationship on an entirely different footing, bring it that much closer to reality, and she was not at all sure she wanted to have a real relationship with this man.

That was something she had not discussed with Joyce. Joyce hadn't said whether she felt the affair she had had was serious, whether it was whole or whether she had just accepted the sex and not bothered at all with establishing a relationship real and true? Difficult to feel serious about someone whose most ardent desire is to pee over you. No worse than someone who ties you to the bed and pretends to be someone else. She was in no position to be morally superior.

All the signs and all her feelings, were that she distinctly did not want anything from him other than what she was already getting. Sex. His sex. Her sex. Her desire to ask him questions was curiosity and she thought, smiling broadly in memory of the beast, she knew what that killed.

She had said she would meet him downstairs and they'd go shopping. She made-up and dressed casually — trousers and sweater, functional underwear and tights. He couldn't have icing on the cake all the time. Too much sugar is bad for the heart.

19

She bought a pair of shoes, he bought a shirt. He helped her choose the shoes. She tried on several pairs, two or three of which she liked, but Martin insisted they did not suit her. Only one of the selection did he approve. She told herself with a fair degree of conviction that this was the pair she liked best too, but it was not entirely true.

He seemed to like the whole process of shopping for clothes. He encouraged her to go into several dress shops and on two occasions made her try on dresses she did not really think she wanted. On the second occasion he came into the changing-room with her. It was so small she had to use his shoulder for balance as she shuffled out of her clothes and into the dress. Before she had done it up the salesgirl pulled the curtain back to ask if she needed any help. When she saw him standing with her she blushed and retreated rapidly.

'She thought we were doing something naughty.'
'Like what?'
'Fucking.'
'Have you ever fucked in a changing-room.'
'No.'

'Do you want to?'
'Now?'
'Yes.'
'I'd love to.'
'Well . . .'
'No.'

They decided the dress was unsuitable and left. The salesgirl gave them a long and disapproving look.

He bought his shirt quickly with little attempt to ask her opinion. She gave it anyway.

They strolled on, hand in hand at times. For all the world a couple. A married couple shopping together on Saturday morning. A domestic routine.

They went to a small restaurant and had a bottle of wine and a large dish of *moules marinière*. It was delicious. Conversation was beginning to flag and Stephanie was glad mussels took a lot of eating. A lot of winkling out and dipping of bread.

He was not giving his 'I'm-so-interested-in-you' performance and nor was he in the 'aren't-you-fascinated-by-me' mood. She was not interested in pulling the teeth of his personality or life nor of elaborating on her own, so in a small and relatively crowded restaurant both resorted to the useful device of actually listening to or pretending to listen to the conversations of other people. She remembered the white-faced girl and the man with the heavy accent that night in the Japanese restaurant. Other people were so much more interesting and anyway most of them she was sure were having real relationships not just passing time before it was respectable or desirable or inevitable to climb back into bed.

Two women talked earnestly but not enough of their conversation was audible to more than guess at the subject.

'. . . And there wasn't much left . . . hardly enough . . . still it was going to happen sure as eggs . . .'

'Do you remember when I . . . that was only, what, last year? Last year I think. It just shows . . . he was doing too much. The whole thing is absurd. I told her . . . I had to tell her . . .'

They listened to another couple much closer, much easer to hear but unfortunately less interesting. The woman wore a wedding ring and, as far as such things are possible to discern, the couple were married and had been married for some considerable time. They talked in little bursts, a subject occurring to one or other of them brought into play and quickly exhausted. Exhausted because they knew already each other's attitude or weren't really interested in the other's reply? But the silences were many. And the difficulty of filling them seemed in inverse proportion to the number of subjects available.

But they were talking she thought, they were out to lunch together. They had their marriage, their relationship and however strange it might seem from the outside it might well work. And she had no grounds for condescension of any sort.

They were on to the coffee, thick black espresso in tiny cups, a brown scum of fine grounds lying on its surface. As she drunk she could feel the diuretic effect and suddenly felt her arse. It felt odd, loose, vaguely numb.

Martin had an extraordinary sixth sense.

'Do you feel sore?'

'No. Not sore.'

'You'd never done it before, had you?'

'No. How could you tell?' How could he tell? There was no hymen of the arsehole, no blood on the sheet. Was it tight? Were women who regularly indulged or allowed him to indulge loose, open with practice? Was his wife?

'Your reaction, I suppose.'

Neatly evaded. She could hardly pursue it in a restaurant where she'd spent the last half hour listening to other people's conversations. A innocent little tête-à-tête about buggery would certainly induce the sort of silence across the room that would make the dropping of a pin infinitely audible.

'Shall we go?'

'Where now?'

'Where do you want to go?'

'Not shopping.'

'Where, then?'

For some reason he wanted her to be the one to suggest going back to the hotel. Since that was what she actually wanted to do most, she satisfied his desire and said it.

Stephanie felt hot and sweaty and ran herself a bath. Not feeling in the least self-conscious she stripped off her clothes and her functional underwear and stood naked in front of him. He was taking his shirt off. She went into the bathroom and climbed into the hot water.

Martin came into the bathroom naked, his penis just slightly erect.

'Shall I dry you?'

She stood and he took a big bath towel and rubbed her vigorously all over. The towel was warm from the heated towel rail. He rubbed her back first then came round to the front ignoring her breasts, except to get them dry, letting them bounce in and out as he moved the towel up and down. It felt lovely, like being dried in front of the fire as a little girl. She opened her legs and he knelt to dry each one then rubbed at her pubic hair until that was more or less dry too. He smiled up at her as he finished, the most friendly smile she had ever seen him give.

They made love quickly but not urgently. She lay on the bed languidly as he kissed her nipples and ran his finger down between her legs finding her clitoris. The soreness made her start at his first touch, but apparently it had no intention of interfering in any significant way and after a while she was only conscious of it as the slightest discomfort. She stroked his now fully erect penis, then held it tightly as he rose above her to come into her. When he was inside her she realised she was only partly liquid though it was only a matter of seconds before her body responded and the friction between them was oiled away.

Perhaps one of the reasons they were so good in bed together was that their minds and their bodies always seemed to want the same thing at the same time. She lay now feeling relaxed and unhurried, feeling almost sleepy. And he clearly felt the same. His movements were quiet, gentle, not pushing. The feeling of being there, of having each other was enough. She lay and just felt him. She used her vaginal muscles to squeeze him, not hard but so she could feel his length, feel his heat, and his hardness.

She wanted to climax but not enough to want to spoil the gentleness; not enough to start frantic movements, not enough to cry and moan and urge. And he felt the same. He moved inside her slowly almost imperceptibly. She allowed her fingers to trail down to his balls touching them with the faintest of pressure; he took one of her breasts in his hand and held it, the nipple pressed into his palm.

Stephanie had idea of how long this lasted. She thought it lasted a long time not because it was unpleasant but because it seemed a long time before the inevitable urgency started to assert itself, before their bodies began to take over from their minds and demand a completion.

She had no idea whether he started moving harder or she did, whether he pushed deeper into her and out again or whether it was her hips reaching off the bed that made him move. She had no idea whether she had reached down to kiss him on the mouth or he had kissed her. She only knew that the laziness was over and they were both caught up in the rhythmic coupling of sex.

It had its own momentum, its own pattern its own heat and its own excitement. This was sex with no images, no fantasies; physical sex, the excitement caused by the nerves situated to send messages of excitement to the cerebral cortex. Reproductive sex; the sex necessary to perpetuate the species if synthetic chemical agents had not been fooling her hormones into thinking it was twenty-eight days of Fridays. (The sex, as he had said, now redundant, no longer necessary.) It was his penis in her cunt, his pubic bone against her clitoris, his chest against her nipples, that made her come. Nothing more. Or her wetness. Her soft vaginal walls clutching his penis, producing the ejaculation in him.

They were too tired for fantasy. Their minds were too tired. Their bodies had not lost the desire, however, and their bodies had decided what they wanted and got it. Now their bodies and their minds wanted rest and they both slept, a long deep sleep.

Stephanie woke easily, not with a start. She became conscious gradually her first thought being what a wonderful sleep she had had. She felt wonderful too, deeply relaxed and satisfied. She could hear by his breathing that he was still asleep next to her. It was twilight and getting dark fast. Across the street from the hotel she could see lights on in other buildings shining out like beacons against he gloom. She closed her eyes again, though not in the least sleepy, just not wanting to give up the feeling of total relaxation by moving. She realised she was starving. She had never had to worry about her weight and had never been tempted to worry about it by the endless adverts hoping to achieve just that. She had never really eaten huge amounts of food, however and had no desire to, which probably explained her figure. But now she was ravenous.

It was an animal existence. The cave of a room. The nest of a bed. The dark outside. The male beast. And raw meat pre-hunted and ready cooked.

Her curiosity about him was increasing within strictly defined limits, of course. It was a curiosity still firmly based on the premise that he was and would ever remain a stranger. It was not a curiosity as to what he would be like on a third wedding anniversary or how he'd be with the children. It was a curiosity that was purely selfish. She wanted to know more about him because she wanted to know more about herself. She had never met a man who moved her so much; consequently knowing more about it would mean finding out more about what moved her. A simple logical proposition.

That was, she told herself, why she was fascinated by questions of his prior sexual experience. She wanted to know if what he had told her was actually true, that what happened between them was a response to each other, an opposite and equal response. If it was not, if he had this facility as a great lover (was lover really the right word?) with all and sundry she would not care;

it would just provide her with a perspective and one she badly needed.

Badly needed? Yes, because she did not believe him. That was it. She did not believe that all that had happened between them was something she had induced, attracted, created, inspired. She just did not believe it. It might be brighter, cleaner, more sparkling with her, but this was a performance he had given before — and not just the once before he had admitted to her at his house. She was merely a better audience, more receptive, more attentive; he was like the stand-up comic who gives a better performance in front of an audience that picks up quickly on all his little throwaways.

Of course, if it was important to her she would have to ask him and be prepared for him to lie. She was sure she would be able to recognise the lie if she asked the right questions.

She had to pee. Moving would undoubtedly wake him but now there was no holding back. As she skirted the bed he woke. She stood for a moment about to apologise but he smiled and said quietly, 'Hallo.'

The hotel had two restaurants and they now dined in the second. He told her that she looked stunning and she believed him. She had taken a great deal of trouble over her appearance tonight and she knew she looked as good as it was possible for her to look.

Martin seemed to be prepared to play the game again; ready to be attentive, talk with bright witty phrases animated with expansive calculated gestures, let his eyes sparkle into hers, respond to her every remark with astonishment, laughter, shock, charm, whatever was appropriate. She enjoyed the game though it was almost impossible for her not to see herself sitting there with him, sitting in this beautiful, exquisitely decorated, extremely expensive restaurant with pink linen tablecloths, fresh flowers on the table, delicate white crockery, as if she was in some complex and fantastic dream, as if the beautiful lady sitting with a napkin on her lap, in her low cut black dress, sheer black stockings and high-heeled black shoes, was actually nothing at all to do with her.

'Would you mind if I asked you something?'

'I might.'

'It's quite important to me. It seems as if it has become quite important to me.'

'What on earth could it be?' He was laughing at her.

'You said what we were like in bed was a reponse, your response to me, my response to you.'

'Yes.'

'That's not true, is it?'

He looked at her, looked straight into her eyes. She imagined he was trying to work out if he could get away with a lie. He obviously decided that he couldn't.

'Not entirely.'

'What part wasn't?'

'Does it matter?'

'In some ways I suppose not . . .'

'Well then.'

'I would just like to know where I stand, that's all. I don't mean stand with you. I mean where I stand in relation to other women.'

'What other women?'

'Other women you've,' she hesitated not wanting to use such a trite word but unable to find another, 'had.'

'On a scale of one to ten.' He was laughing again.

'No. No, that's not what I mean, and you know it.'

'Do I?'

'You now exactly what I mean.'

'I'm afraid I don't.'

'You're being obtuse then.'

'You want to know what I've done with other women?'

'Yes.'

'I told you there was another woman . . .'

'And the others?'

'Whether I've done the sort of things we've done?'

'Yes.'

'Tell me why it matters so much to you. You enjoy it, don't you? Why on earth does it matter whether it's happened before? Make me understand that.'

'It matters . . . Since you came to my flat, then at your house. I've never felt like this about anyone sexually. Sexually. I'm not in love with you. A lot of women, would confuse what you've made me feel with love. I know it's not. I'm sure that I've loved anyone but I'm certain that I've never felt the things you've made me feel. You made me feel a part of me that I've never really had much to do with before; just went through the motions. It's like having been paralysed from the waist down; feeling the sensations come back, wanting to walk, run, swim and all at the same time. I just want to know why.'

He laughed again. 'What am I supposed to say? Because I'm a great lover?'

'If that's true.'

'I don't think it is. I just think the things I like doing obviously affect you.'

'And other women?'

'Why are you so interested in other women?'

'I want to know.'

'What I said to you was true. You respond to me.'

'Have other women responded to you too?'

'Yes.'

The answer depressed her immediately though she

had known that if he told her the truth that would be his answer. 'Every woman?'

'No. I haven't done it with many.'

'Every one you've tried?'

'No.'

'How many?'

'You want a percentage?'

'Yes.' She was cross, angry at his smug smiling face.

'I couldn't begin to say.'

'Try.'

'No.'

'Please tell me how many you've tied to the bed, how many have begged you to do it again?' Hearing what she had said, suddenly realised someone else might have heard. She looked round. No one appeared to be taking notice.

'What is this?'

'You must have some idea.'

'Look don't you think . . .'

'Don't be modest. Modesty isn't your forté. Come on, seventy per cent, eighty?'

'I have no idea. Why on earth are you so cross? You're the one who brought this subject up. Now you're cross. I don't understand.'

'Don't you?'

'No.'

'You still haven't answered.'

'And I have no intention of answering. I don't know what the hell's the matter with you. Why can't you just leave it? What does it matter? What I've done with other women has nothing to do with you or with us. For God's sake what happens in bed between us is just between us. Nobody else. You must know that. You said I've made you feel things you've never felt before. Isn't that enough?'

She realised that she couldn't push it any further unless she was prepared to finish it all here and now, walk out before the coffee, go to the room and pack. Is that what she wanted to do? Not for half a second. He had told her what she wanted to know anyway, hadn't he.

The mood had been broken. He was not prepared to play the game any more and though she tried to indulge in small talk he was not receptive. He ordered large brandies. The drink made him more morose. He appeared to show no sign of wanting to go to the room and as the restaurant emptied suggested they transferred to the hotel bar which she suspected, rightly, was an excuse for another large drink.

They sat on tall bar stools. The way her dress was cut, it was difficult not to show a good deal of leg. He seemed fascinated by it staring down into her lap. He moved a fold of the material aside to reveal the top of her black stocking.

'That's so exciting.'

She made no attempt to cover herself again. 'I'm glad you still think so.'

'Are you?'

'Yes.'

'I got the impression you wouldn't be.'

'I'd like to go to the room now.'

'Oh, would you?'

'Do we need this charade? Or don't you want me any more?'

'My dear, you are a very sexy woman.' He laughed. 'On a scale of one to . . .'

'Don't.'

On a sale of one to ten how did she rate when it came to being buggered, revealed to room-service waiters, and all the other games?

'Let's go then.'

'I haven't finished my drink,' he said.

She covered her leg.

'Have you thought how far you'd go?' He looked straight into her eyes as he asked the question.

'How far I'd go?' she repeated.

'Where you would draw the line?' He was looking at her intently, his eyes unblinking.

Stephanie thought about the question seriously. It astonished her that she actually had no idea of the answer.

'I don't know,' she said honestly.

'For example, if the stranger had been real?'

If the stranger had been real? If the punishment had been real? The pain? She had thought about it before, provoked by a passage from one of The Books.

They had tied her to a metal ring screwed into the wooden beam that ran across the room just below the ceiling. Her wrists had been bound with a long rope which was pulled through the ring until she could only touch the floor by standing on tiptoe and stretching as hard as she could. She was naked and not bound in any other way.

It was a bamboo cane like they used in schools. The man delivered the first blow across her buttocks, the woman the second and they continued to alternate. The man's strokes were harder and bit deeper into her flesh. The woman couldn't hit as hard but placed her strokes in areas that seemed to hurt more, the top of the thighs, back and front, and the small of the back.

They had placed a mirror so she could see the welts that appeared in her flesh. When they had finished and left her moaning and dangling, still bound to the ring, her buttocks were criss-crossed with long thin bruises.

The Books had raised the questions, given her a vocabulary but Martin had freed her sexual imagination. He made her realise how sexual fantasy could become reality. He had created a new dimension for her. An entirely new dimension like a sixth sense. A dimension in which anything was possible. A dimension which fed and nourished the other dimensions of reality.

She knew that she did not want the stranger to be real. Not the reality of the dirty foul-smelling tramp that she had imagined. She did not want that stranger. But in the other dimension, across the divide, there were other strangers, other ideas. There were things she knew she would do now that she would never have done before. Do and enjoy. Enjoy the pain. Enjoy the pleasure.

He was trying to provoke her. If she did not reply now and let the subject drop, that would be an end of it. If she did not reply there could be no question later that it was not her responsibility. If she sat there now, sipped her drink again, dismissed his provocation, and said absolutely nothing more, the whole thing would disappear into the wide and misty realms of fantasy, unrealised, unfulfilled fantasy. But on the other hand, if she said . . .

'Would you like it?'

Of course he would like it; he was the provocateur.

'It might be interesting.' If he had wanted to sound non-committal, as if bored with the subject, he did not succeed.

'I can think of all sorts of interesting things.'

Her dress was a perfect accomplice. The material of

her skirt fell away to reveal the top of the black stocking again. For the first time one of the other men at the bar could see her legs. He stared, ignoring his companion. She made no attempt to cover herself.

'What's the most interesting?'

He had finished his brandy. He looked down into her lap and put his hand on her exposed knee. His hand moved up to the top of her stocking and then moved around until it found the bud of her suspender. The other man watched intently. She watched the other man.

'You could make it come true.' She did not smile as she said it.

20

Earlier Stephanie had chosen her underwear carefully and made sure she had put it on in the bathroom so he wouldn't see. Her acquisition of lingerie in the last few weeks had been unwonted. And this was the most expensive underwear she had ever bought. A white silk camisole top and matching french knickers and suspender belt. The three items were beautifully cut and heavily embellished with delicate lace. The silk was so fine it had a slight sheen. She knew she looked quite wonderful in it.

Now she took her dress off in the bathroom and came back into the bedroom in the underwear. He was suitably impressed. He stood and kissed her full on the mouth while his hands caressed her and the silk from the back. She could feel his erection grow with gratifying reliability and press into her navel. He had already taken his shirt off and now she broke away from him and undid his belt and unzipped his fly.

Martin was still slightly drunk, she thought, and when he had come back into the room he had poured them both brandies from the drinks fridge. His brandy she saw had already been consumed. Now he flopped back on to the bed and she pulled his pants and trousers off. His penis was erect but not fully; it looked like a giant slug trying to stand upright. From some dim and distant and obviously well-informed sex education class she remembered the teacher explaining that male organs were very different sizes in their flaccid state but when fully erect the size difference decreased dramatically. Speaking statistically, of course, Devlin being the exception to every rule.

She imagined the booze was inhibiting his reactions to her appearance. That was disappointing. It was also her fault. Her fault for arguing with him. Her fault for trying to behave as though their relationship was normal. She stood by his head looking down at him, letting him look at her. Then she slipped off the camisole so her large breasts quivered into his view. The effect was negligible. So much for expensive underwear. That was a waste of money.

'Well?'

'You don't seem interested.'

'You look beautiful.'

'Do you want to sleep?'

'No. You have to tell me what you want me to do.'

She wondered afterwards if everything he had done to her had been stage-managed to get to this point. She wondered if everything he had ever done with all the other women was stage-managed to get them to this point, to get them to invent, create, expand some fantastic sexual rite. That was Martin's excitement. How many refused? How many had nothing to contribute to his play? She seemed to be obsessed with percentages tonight.

If she was being manipulated, if this was a situation he had created, it had taken her no time to fall in with his plans. Total compliance. She supposed it had taken such a short time because it was exactly what she wanted, and exactly what she had expected from this weekend. She had known things would happen to her; to be honest she had hoped things would happen to her that were quite outside her experience. That was why she'd gone along. The experience of Martin was something total, something that could not be taken in pieces, agreeing to some and not others.

Of course that was all sophisticated rationalisation. He was not actually manipulating her. She was doing nothing she did not want to do. She had become greedy the more she thought about it. Sexually greedy. She wanted more. She did not know where the line was drawn but she was determined to find out — if there was a line at all.

She had never done anything as daring in her life. Daring was the wrong word, she decided. It implied frivolity, like wearing an especially revealing dress. This was brave. It was brave because she was doing something she had invented, something she wanted, something frightening but exciting — the correlation between fright and excitement was something she understood but had never experienced before — and something carried on by and only by, her own volition. Volition and will. The Nietzsche of the bedroom.

And she no longer knew, and no longer cared, which of her thoughts were rationalisations of her absurd or crude or unconscionable behaviour. There was just behaviour and she couldn't seriously tell herself that without a rationale she would be behaving any differently. Not now.

As a matter of pure fact there was no alternative anyway. She had told him what she wanted and he'd responded immediately. He had asked no questions, shown no reaction. This was after all, what he wanted, wasn't it? Her secret. It was not a fantasy she had worked on, refined, masturbated over. It was instant. But no less exciting.

Now it was too late for second thoughts. A few minutes after he had left Stephanie had tried to free herself. For one moment she had wanted to be free. For one moment she seriously wanted to be free and she tried to pull her hands out of the straps that held them to the chair. She could not. Fortunately her serious desire to be free did not persist and she settled for the fact that her bonds were real. Freedom was academic.

Her instructions had become his, her orders no longer part of her.

He had told her to sit, in the white silk underwear, on one of the upright chairs. Martin handed her the camisole and she slipped it back over her head. The seat of the chair was upholstered in a rough tweedy material, heavy-duty for heavy wear, which felt itchy against the naked flesh of her thighs, the delicate silk provided little protection for her bottom. The wooden front legs of the chair rose up past the seat and was jointed at right angles across the top to meet the back legs and form arms, the back legs also supporting the backrest of the chair.

On every previous occasion he had blindfolded her before anything else. Stephanie had said she did not want a blindfold now. He opened the black case and removed two small leather straps, using them to secure her wrists to the arms of the chair at the front. She had watched as he took two more straps from the case and used these on her ankles, binding them to the front legs of the chair. His erection returned while he worked.

He had dressed casually as though going for a walk in the country. He had made no attempt to look at her.

He carried on as if she had ceased to exist. She said nothing. She felt the harsh material of the chair against her back and bottom and shifted slightly in the chair.

He had left without saying a word. As she could not see the door of the bedroom she listened to see if he had put the 'Do Not Disturb' sign on the door. She could hear nothing. He had turned out the light so the only light was from the street outside and below. She shifted in her chair again.

There was no way of hiding from herself that she was terribly excited. She could feel all the physical signs; her pulse rate was faster, her breathing shallower, her erect nipples pushed out against the silk of the camisole, and though there was no way of telling, she felt that her cunt was hot and very wet.

She tested the straps again, not in any attempt to get free but to feel them, to remind herself of the situation, to feel that shiver of sensation as she failed to move her arms or legs. To know again that he would come back and she would be powerless. Why was it so exciting? She had no idea nor cared that she had none. The feeling was enough.

She could see, across the room in the gloom, the reflection of her shape, bound in the chair, in the wardrobe mirror. She could not see her face but she could see the whole silhouette. *Bound Lady in a Chair.* A sculpture. A living sculpture. Living Art.

This was the most dangerous thing she had ever done. Because of that it was also the most exciting. That had to be true. She supposed a point might come, and come quite soon, when the danger (did she mean physical danger, or mental danger, or both, or were they the same?) would swamp the excitement, put it out like a bucket of water thrown over a lighted match. And there would be no way to light the match ever again. Or perhaps the match would burn all the way through?

Stephanie concentrated on what she felt. The mild discomfort of sitting partly dressed on coarse material; the slight constriction around her ankles and wrists, a tingling sensation where the blood had to force its way past the straps, the tightness of her nipples. She tried to open her legs slightly to get some idea of how her cunt was reacting. She would have liked to slip her hand down into her pubic hair and feel the hot dampness. The fact that she couldn't, the fact that she was not free to touch herself, caused a sharp bite of pleasure again.

The door opened. She peered across the room. It was not Martin. The harsh overhead light was switched on. A room-service waiter, short white starched waiter jacket, black trousers, looking for a used food tray in the wrong room and finding a great deal more than he was looking for. The pass key was frozen in his hand as he looked at her. He looked at her once, looked away, then stared at her, finding it hard to believe his eyes. Coming closer, looking closer. Says something under his breath in Spanish or Italian. She remains silent, feeling a bead of sweat run down from her armpit until absorbed by the silk camisole. There is nothing she can say, nothing she can think of to say. He stares. Seeing her breasts through the white silk, looking up her stockinged legs. Looking, then leering, a glint of large white teeth. Walking round the back of the chair, for a moment, like a child in a wonderland of toys, not knowing which to play with first. Checking the bonds on her wrists as if to make sure they're real, not some wicked trick. Cupping her breasts in his hands, leaning over her. She smells the stench of his body odour, the foul smell of whisky on his breath. Nothing she can do to stop him squeezing her breasts, pinching her nipples, pinching them hard, trying to make her cry out; or pulling her knickers down to her knees and pushing his dirty calloused hands into the soft folds of her cunt. Not bothering to find a way through the pubic hair, just pushing through it, trapping it, pushing some into her cunt. Brittle hair against soft wet flesh.

Then walking round the front of the chair. She sees his trousers shiny with wear, the short jacket fraying at the edges with too much washing, too much ironing and instant starch. He speaks in Spanish or Italian again, this time to her, a question.

His English didn't extend to such situations, only to restaurants. 'More haricot verte, madam?' 'How would you like your steak cooked?' It couldn't run to 'You're going to suck me off.' He repeated the question. She looked at him, looked into his eyes. He looked away immediately but for a second their eyes had met. She had seen the lust and the fear and the uncertainty. But lust was uppermost. Unzipping his trousers. Pulling his penis out. Wanking himself until he was hard. Taking her head in his hands, holding her cheeks, centring her mouth like a target for his arrow. Leaning towards her awkwardly because of the chair.

She swallowed him greedily, guzzled him, covered his penis with the wetness of her mouth, the heat of her mouth. Making her mouth like her cunt. Greedy for him. Greedy to feel the sperm splash out of him into her throat. Feel it gush out hard and hit the back of her throat. Feel his hands pulling her face on to him, trying to lift her from the chair to which she was bound. The bonds preventing him getting to her, preventing her swallowing him deeper, longer.

Stephanie had no idea how long he had been gone. She opened her eyes as he came in. He did not put the light on at the door but waited until he got into the room and put the bedside light on. She imagined that he had brought a woman, that she was standing in the little corridor by the door, the only area of the room she could not see. He came over to her and kissed her very gently on the mouth, the tenderest kiss he had ever given her in their short relationship. Was it a kiss of apology he couldn't find a woman? Was it a kiss to ask whether she wanted to go on? There was no question in his eyes.

He had brought a woman. He walked to the little corridor by the door and led her into the room holding her by the elbow.

'Alice,' he said for no reason she could think of.

It had happened. She took a long deep breath. It had happened. Her secret. Her new secret.

The woman was older than Stephanie, at least she looked older. She wore very little make-up. Her dark brown hair was cut short and well-shaped. She wore a trenchcoat, under which was a V-necked purple sweater, a black leather pencil skirt that reached to her knees. He helped her take off the trenchcoat and hang it on the back of the door. An obvious image of a prostitute, a film-maker's image with less make-up.

Stephanie felt the excitement of anticipation grow as Alice looked at her. The questions leapt up in her mind and her body. Her body was quivering with sensation, her mind was pulling out the file cards of queries. Was she a prostitute? Where had he got her? How much had he had to pay? How long for? How did he know where to go? Because he knew where to go, did that mean he used prostitutes regularly.

Was this woman a prostitute? My God, perhaps it

was his wife? His wife. Was this fantasy, so conveniently arranged, not something she had invented but something pushed on to her by him? Something he created, something they created, their game, their fantasy, their fulfilment? He had made her respond, made her make the right choice, made her want what he wanted, they wanted, as he had before. As he'd made her want the other games, now he'd created this one and made her want it, made her ask for it. Part of the grand strategy. To please his wife. To pander for his wife. His wife's revenge on her husband's mistresses. His wife's answer. His wife's way of coping.

'What do you want me to do?' Alice asked.

'I told you.'

'This is what she wants?'

'Yes.'

The first touch of her hand was a physical shock. Alice touched her shoulder, moving her hand to hold her by the upper arm. He sat down on the bed in a good position to watch. Stephanie closed her eyes and felt her blood racing. The questions would have to wait.

Alice's hand slipped to the back of her neck and pulled her head upward as she kissed Stephanie on the mouth. She had never felt a woman's mouth before. It was full of new sensation, softnesses and hardnesses in different places, different planes, different angles. She immediately lost herself in the female mouth. Lost herself in the exploration. Alice seemed not to mind, she did not move to end the kiss but let it go on and on.

If this was his fantasy, his invention, she knew it perfectly matched her own. If it was not, her fantasy was perfect in itself.

Alice was kneading her breast as the kiss continued. Not gently but strong hard movements. Then breaking the kiss she came round the back of the chair and worked on both breasts together, crumpling the white silk until she pulled it up and sunk her fingers into the abundant naked flesh.

It had always seemed completely logical to her that only a woman would know a woman's body. Only a woman would know the special places, the knots of sensation, the places to touch lightly, the places to knead and squeeze; only a woman would know the rhythms and tempos of a woman's body. This knowledge she had left happily at the back of her mind, unchallenged and unexplored. She had never connected it with the thought that she might like to have a woman touch and knead and squeeze and find her rhythms. Not until now. Not until Martin had come along and had invented the situation, found the woman.

Alice stopped and came round the front of the chair to look at her. They looked into each other's eyes. Stephanie could tell nothing about Alice from her eyes. She could not tell what she was, why she was here, who she was. The eyes contained nothing but mild curiosity, not the sort of curiosity one would feel for some dumb creature caught in a particularly unsubtle and obvious trap. She felt it was more than that. It was a curiosity as to the feeling more than the reason. Not why she was doing this but how it felt. How it felt to be tied in a chair while a perfect stranger mauled and prodded you.

Still looking into her eyes, Alice knelt in front of the chair and, pushing passed the crotch of her knickers, found the opening of her vagina, the moist hot opening, with her fingertip. Making a tiny piston of one finger she moved it back and forth. After a few minutes of this she transferred the finger upwards, rearranging the crotch of the knickers to accommodate the movement, until it touched her clitoris. Touched it, then stroked it, then pressed against it, then gently flicked against it, then alternated all three things.

Stephanie had no idea she was going to have an orgasm until the first obvious signs had started. They surprised her. But there was no doubt now that an orgasm was coming. She looked down at Alice's head as it peered intently into her lap, she rocked against the straps wanting the feeling of constraint to add to the other feelings that were making her come. She moaned softly almost hoping Alice would look up. She saw him look up from where he sat on the bed watching Alice. Saw him look at her. Then she closed her eyes, not out of choice but because she had to give in to the sensation and her sight was no longer required by the engine inside her that was driving her forward, pushing her on to a sharp sudden release.

When she opened her eyes again — it was probably only a few seconds later but it might have been hours — Alice was standing taking off the V-necked sweater. She wore a very ordinary black bra of stretchy elastic. She unzipped the black leather skirt and stepped out of it. Her knickers were just as functional as the bra, white and cotton with the elastic around the top frayed in places. She wore neither stockings nor tights.

Hardly the stuff of fantasy. Weren't prostitutes meant to wear black satin basques, long ruched suspenders and tiny knickers of exquisite lace? Another cliché. Alice was helping Martin take his shirt off. He didn't say anything to her, just allowed her to unbutton the shirt and take it off and stood so that she could undo his belt and pull his trousers off. When she had pulled them to the floor he stepped out of them. Couldn't get his socks off first this time, she thought. She had left his pants on. His erection was complete. His penis peeped from the top of his pants like the drawings of Chad peeping over the wall, as if it was asking could it join in, any room for one eye?

As far as she could tell, none of the undressing, not even her peeling his socks off as he sat on the bed, indicated any sort of intimacy between them.

Martin unclipped her bra. Alice had small breasts and they were not well shaped. Surprisingly, they looked like the breasts of an older woman, slightly wrinkled and flaccid as though they had once been full and ripe but now were emptied and dry. And out of all proportion, the nipples were small and very pink. On the other hand her arse was magnificent — nature's compensation? Two halves perfectly rounded, perfect symmetry from waist to the top of her thigh. Not a trace of fat or wrinkle or blemish of any kind. The curves of a crescent moon.

Alice had taken off her knickers. Her pubic hair was soft, babylike and formed a neat pattern, all the hairs lying downward and inward pointing to the apex of their triangle, as though she combed it into shape. He noticed the pattern too and reached out to confirm it with his hand, stroking from the outer hairs down into her lap.

They did not kiss. Stephanie remembered reading that prostitutes did not kiss. Any other intimacy was permitted but kissing was forbidden. It had always seemed to her to have a strange logic. There was something about the head that was sacred; it was too near the mind to be able to isolate. You could isolate your cunt, isolate your nipples, let them belong to someone else, cut off the messages from the nerves because they had such a long way to travel, so many places where they could be blocked and sidetracked. But not the mouth. Only inches for the messages to leap.

But Alice had kissed her because she liked women, because that was her pleasure not her job. Men were her job.

He lay back on the bed his legs open and Alice knelt between them. She took his penis into her mouth, plunging up and down on it with an almost manic frequency, her head bobbing to and fro. Then she withdrew and started licking his penis, licking it ferociously like a child with a lollipop trying to eat it before it melted away.

Stephanie watched from the prison of the chair. The sight did not arouse her or repel her. As the chair was directly opposite the foot of the bed she had a perfect view of Alice's bottom, stretched tight and divided by the long slit of her cunt and the downy pubic hair on either side of the long labia which came into view as she dipped her head further down into his crotch.

She did not feel any jealousy. Nor did she particularly feel that she wanted to be on the bed with them. Trying to be as accurate as she could about her feelings she supposed that she wanted Alice to be touching her again, and not him. Or for him to be touching her. That was it, she felt neglected.

Her bonds were no longer exciting. Now they were annoying, irritating; she wanted to be free of them. She wanted to touch Alice. She wanted to experience Alice, wanted to know what it was like to touch a woman, what her strange breasts felt like, what her tiny nipples felt like, what it would be like to kiss those delicately haired labia and press herself against Alice's cunt.

Stephanie knew that she could not say anything. The rules were very strict on that point and since they were her rules she alone knew how strict. She could moan, though. Moan and wriggle in the chair. Moan and wriggle. Moan and wriggle until Alice looked back over her shoulder to take notice and Martin sat up to look at her.

'She wants some attention,' Alice said.

'I'll untie her.'

'Do you want that?'

Stephanie made no reply to the question. Perhaps, unconsciously her head nodded minutely.

'I wish I had breasts like hers.'

I wish I had an arse like yours, Stephanie thought.

'Let her wait.' Martin's voice seemed harsh.

'I want her.'

You are not supposed to want, you are only supposed to do.

'What about me?'

'There's room for you,' protested Alice.

'Let her wait.'

'I don't want to wait.' It was a surprising thing for Alice to say. *You are supposed to wait.*

Alice got up from the bed. As she did he got up on to his knees and grabbed her hand, pulling her round to him, pulling her lips on to his, using his other hand to press her head down on to his mouth. Breaking all the rules. Alice did not resist. She kissed him back, wrapping her arms round his naked body and pushing her tongue deep into his mouth.

They released her together. Alice stood, her pubic hair brushing the knuckle of one hand as she unstrapped the other; Martin knelt and freed her ankles.

Freedom was difficult to cope with at first. She felt still welded to the chair. She felt unsure, uncertain what to do now she had a choice again. For quite some time she had sat in the chair passively because she could do nothing else. She did not have to choose whether to get up, whether to dress or undress, move kiss, touch, allow. She had been an object with no will. A thing to be done to, or not. And that, after all, was what she had wanted. Then. That was what she had asked for and got. That, that idea, that unfreedom, had been what had excited her. Excited her with him.

Now Stephanie could decide. She could decide to walk over to the bed. She could decided to put his penis in her mouth, take Alice's breast in her hand, pull Alice's legs apart and taste the juices from her cunt. She could decide, and for a moment the choices were overwhelming. For a moment the newness of it was like a sexual feeling, like a wave of delicious sensation, a tongue thrust into her ear, or mouth or cunt. The pleasure of anticipation.

The anticipation made sharper by the situation. Because she knew there would be no anti-climax. The fantasy would be bettered by reality. The anticipation would be bettered by the participation.

Alice had kissed him. He had surprised her admittedly, but she had kissed him back, kissed him hard. And said she didn't want to wait.

Martin had gone to the bathroom. He had not closed the door and she could hear the faint noise of him peeing. Alice sat on the edge of the bed. Stephanie got up rather unsteadily — her mind and body in the same state — and walked towards her. Almost before she realised what had happened she was standing in Alice's arms. Alice kissed her navel, then tenderly and gently pressed her cheek against it as though listening for some inner pregnant life. Her hands were caressing her buttocks and thighs.

Stephanie had to remind herself she was no longer tied, no longer passive, that she must participate now, that she was required to touch and move and be.

She pressed Alice's head to her navel with both hands, feeling the dark brown hair thick and silky under her fingers. Then she knelt and took Alice's cheeks in her hands and kissed her, pushing her tongue into her mouth and kissing her with all the gentleness she could muster, trying to communicate with her kiss, trying to tell Alice the situation. And trying to feel back from Alice what she thought and knew. Their mouths were bad communicators. Impressions were muddled and indistinct. There was a tenderness, there was a proper feeling, something more than sexual excitement and desire, more than lust. But whether it was more than Alice's obvious delight in a woman, more than Alice's love for and care for women in general, her ease with and liking and desire for women it was impossible to tell.

(If she was a prostitute he would be frightened of catching a disease. Is that why he had not fucked her? Is that why she had only sucked him? Could you catch a disease from another woman?)

Stephanie knew she wanted Alice. Wanted to take her, fuck her, be like a man with her. Wanted it suddenly and unexpectedly. She pushed Alice back on to the bed. They lay full length, still kissing, their bodies pressed against each other, their legs twined around each other to lever their bodies closer. Through the white silk she felt the softness of Alice's body and the hardness. Felt the hard pubic bone against her own and her breasts pressed against Alice's ribcage. She could not feel Alice's breasts. She tightened her arms around Alice's back, trying to feel her breasts against her, but she only became more aware of her own, balloonlike flesh pushing up to escape the squeezing vice of chests.

It was Alice who stripped off the camisole and the french knickers, who carefully pulled off the stockings and unclipped the suspender belt.

He had come back from the bathroom but did not attempt to join them on the bed. He sat in a chair.

She caught his eye. He almost smiled. He was not watching them intently like a voracious Peeping Tom. Is that what she expected, wide-eyed with saliva drooling from the side of his mouth, craning his head so as not to miss the most intimate contact.

Alice was kissing her again. The feeling of their two bodies lying against each other naked for the first time, warm and lush, suddenly made her feel sharply, hungrily sexy, made her heart beat faster, and her breathing shallower. Made her want Alice — whatever want meant.

As she had never wanted a woman before, as there was no penetration involved, she supposed it meant giving her an orgasm. Wanting a man was so specific. He could be enclosed, wrapped around, taken in. Had. Literally had. Taken in and milked. Discarded when dry.

But there was no such specific with a woman. In a way her desire to 'have' Alice was only an expression of a desire to come herself, since the two things were equal and the same. She supposed that she should make Alice come by kissing her, sucking her clitoris and fingering her cunt. But actually she had no idea. It had never occurred to her before. That was true. She knew she wanted this woman, wanted everything this woman could do to her and everything she could do to this woman, knew that the feelings she had and would have were exquisite and like nothing she had ever experienced with a man — at least partly — and yet at the same time what was happening was something she had never dreamt of and, more surprisingly perhaps, would never want or dream of again. Or was that just a comforting thought.

He was involved. He was sitting in the chair and watching. He was Alice. She was not a closet lesbian because he was Alice. Alice on her own was . . . interesting. But Alice with him — the difference was total. Or was that another rationalisation? Another convenient excuse. Just to put her mind at rest. Just to shove her experience into some convenient little niche where it wouldn't bother her too much or even at all. Let him take all the blame. For the time being.

It didn't matter anyway. She could sort it all out later, she had to. If she didn't then so much the better.

Alice was kissing her breast, moulding it into a peak with both her hands and sucking her nipple. Sucking it hard, using her teeth to bite. Making her gasp with that odd mixture of pleasure and pain, the pain lingering when the teeth had gone only to turn almost instantly to a warm ache of pleasure. The other breast now. The same thing. Moulding, squeezing it together then the teeth pinching at the nipple. The other, now untouched, nipple still felt the pleasure principle. Both together somehow connected, the two parts together were greater than the sum of both.

As Alice kissed her navel she wormed round so she could find Alice's breasts. She could not give them the same treatment; there was not enough to squeeze but she bit on the nipple and heard Alice moan. And she felt Alice's mouth on her pubic hair now and then her tongue on her clitoris. And she moved down and saw Alice's legs part to welcome her into the unison of action.

She treated Alice's cunt as if it were her own. Remembering all the things she had wanted to tell men to do to her, how to kiss and suck or stroke with their tongues, how to use their saliva, how to use their fingers. And Alice did the same to her.

Alice reached back and caught a nipple in her fingers, pinching it again. Alice's tongue stroked and probed. She did the same to Alice. Their orgasms nearer. She could feel Alice's orgasm. Feel it approaching. Taste it. Feel it in her mouth, against her tongue, under her fingers. Feel it vibrating against her body, vibrating in her breasts. Feel it so close to her that it was impossible to tell if it were Alice's or her own. Equal and the same. She wanted her orgasm and wanted Alice's. She wanted to come quickly. She increased the pressure on Alice's clitoris with her tongue, increased the rhythm of her fingers pressed into Alice's cunt, rocked her body against Alice's, and felt Alice do the same. Felt Alice's mouth and tongue and fingers. Felt Alice's rhythm harder and stronger and faster. And felt this bring her to spill over the top of orgasm, as she felt Alice do the same; and Alice doing the same kicked her further on, deeper into the pleasure knowing the circle was complete and this vibration would in turn feed Alice and Alice feed her.

The orgasm didn't stop. It didn't seem to stop. The blood still rushed through her eyes blurring vision, accentuating the images of sex, breasts, cunts, arses, thighs, making Stephanie hot and wet, making her grab up at his penis as he came to stand by the bed as if it was the pommel of an American saddle and she was about to swing into the seat. Making her stuff it into her mouth, gobble it up, then pull him down on to the bed and sit on it with her cunt until she felt he was buried so deep and so far he would never dig his way out. And Alice was there too, Alice's orgasm, like her own, going on, sending waves of electricity through her and through him. Alice kissing her breasts. Alice kissing her mouth. Alice kissing him. Feeling Alice through him. The same circle. The same circle with

Martin in the centre; revolving around him. Or were they revolving around her. Or Alice.

Alice's cunt sitting on his mouth. She had his penis inside her while he licked and sucked at Alice's cunt. She could see his tongue, see how it made Alice squirm and feel. There was no question now of building to an orgasm. She was having one long continuous orgasm. The only question was to make it last. Everything had to be done quickly, urgently so it would not die. Everything had to be instant. The fire consumed, feeding on itself, feeding on sensation, images, fantasies. The touch of a woman's mouth on her breast, his penis inside her cunt, his mouth between Alice's thighs. Rocking together. A chain of feeling. Alice reaching to hold the stem of his penis at the bottom of her cunt. Pressing herself down on his penis so hard and so deep Stephanie could feel his balls against her labia, feel Alice's fingers holding him. And then Alice's finger, finally it seemed but it may not have been, feeling Alice's finger caressing the huge stem of his penis, caressing it in long slow pulls from tip to base, caressing it as Alice pushed her finger up alongside his penis in Stephanie's cunt.

Feeling his sperm rise in his penis, watching the pictures in her mind as the door opened and Devlin walked in naked holding his erection in one hand to prevent it knocking against the furniture, and Alice's finger pressing against him as though holding the sperm back. Alice's mouth opening to kiss her as she lent forward, her eyes wild, her mouth slack, both of them sucking on either side of Devlin's penis, kissing each other by kissing him, trying to get at each other's mouth by devouring him, freeing his sperm to spurt out, hot and hard, each jet pounding against their naked bodies and on Martin, spurt after spurt. An endless stream rtin spunked too, as Alice's mouth kissed hers, evlin stood, his penis slashed through the painting of the woman, crimson oil paint staining the gnarled and veined flesh.

Only Devlin was imagined.
The rest was real.

Stephanie was lying on her back, her legs drawn up, her knees bent. Martin knelt in front of her facing her open cunt; not touching it, not looking, his eyes glazed and sightless. She twisted around to look at Alice who stood by the bed. They looked into each other's eyes for a long time but said nothing.

21

She had been sore for a week. The most irritating part of this was not the pain but the fact that suddenly grazing her arm across her chest or crossing her legs without thinking reminded her instantly of the cause of the discomfort. Reminded her of what she had done.

It was not that she wanted to forget. It was just that she didn't want to be reminded at the wrong moments, didn't want to be reminded unexpectedly when she was not ready to deal with the memory. It needed to be dealt with. It wiped everything else out of her mind, pulled her back to the hotel, the bed, the chair, Alice, Martin.

She discovered that little pieces of cotton wool in her bra helped her nipples, but she could find nothing to ease the soreness around her clitoris. Only time.

After two weeks, with the soreness gone, she was relatively safe from unexpected recollection. She had seen Martin in the lift one lunchtime and spent the whole afternoon and evening in that peculiar half-life that absent-mindedness produces. After that she had decided she must pull herself together and cope.

If she sat alone at night and thought about what had

ed, thought calmly and rationally, the result was s the same. No justification, no rationalisation, ... feeling of a chapter closed, a new awareness. Just a rather sickly feeling of sexual excitement and an absolute determination that under no circumstances must she ever see Martin again.

She did not allow George to make love to her. At first she told him she was not in the mood, then, on the second occasion when he started towards her to kiss and maul, she told him it was her period and then, finally, she told him the truth. She didn't want to have sex with him again. And the one thing that had to be said for George was that he did take no for an answer. Rejection was his forté.

Devlin didn't. Devlin phoned and continued to phone despite her refusals to go out with him or see him or even, in the end, talk to him. In a funny way she knew she would see Devlin again. But not at the moment. At the moment men and sex were out. For that matter women and sex were out too, the rider being necessary these days. She was disappointed in herself, she decided. Disappointed she had not run screaming and naked through the hotel foyer. Disappointed she had played his game. Disappointed that she still did not know if it had been his game or whether in truth, it had been her game too. Disappointed that, at the moment, she could not admit to herself that it did not matter who Alice was or what she was. Disappointed that she still wanted to know.

She had read up on venereal disease and since she was not sure in her memory of the tangle of organs and limbs who had touched who and with what she had gone to a clinic for a blood test. It was clear. That being so, she wished desperately that she could have been sure who had fucked who and in what order.

Though Alice not having VD might only prove that Alice was a clean prostitute.

It was three weeks later when Martin phoned.

'I've been a stranger. I'm sorry.'

He had never apologised before. She did not reply.

'Are you cross with me?'

'No.'

'Good.'

'You sound cross.'

She was not cross. She was out of breath and hot. Her face was flushed but she was not cross.

'I'm not.'

'I've missed you.' He did not say it tenderly.

'Have you?'

'Obviously not mutual.'

She wanted to reply, and thought about doing so but when it came to it she did not honestly know whether the answer was 'yes' or 'no'. He took her silence to mean no.

'Sorry to have bothered you.'

'What did you want?'

'It doesn't matter.'

'I didn't mean . . .'

'What?'

'I don't know what to say.'

'I was ringing to ask if you wanted to see me again.'

She laughed. A release of tension.

'Why are you laughing?'

' "See" seems such a ludicrous euphemism in the circumstances.'

'Would you rather I said fuck?'

She was smiling now, grinning from ear to ear. 'Is that what you mean?'

'You know what I mean.'

'You never answer my questions.'

e are so many. Next Tuesday. I'll pick you up eight.'

It was Friday. Three days to call it off. Three days to think about calling it off. Three days to think and wonder and weigh the risks, the problems, the difficulties. To ask herself what she was doing and what she had done.

The truth was simple however. She knew she wanted to play safe (better safe than sorry), take no more risks, no more scares, no more excitements. She knew Martin was not safe, represented risk, had taken her into areas she had never dreamt she would be willing to go. She knew all that. So the truth was simple. She would be waiting for him on Tuesday as breathless and exhilarated as she had been the first time. Waiting to see where he would take her. Waiting to see where she wanted to go. Her secret.